ABOUT THE AUTHOR

Sundari Venkatraman is an Indie Author who has 64 books to her credit. These books have consistently featured in the Top 100 Bestseller Lists on Amazon Kindle, in both romance as well as Asian Drama categories. Her latest hot romances have all been on #1 Bestseller slot in Amazon India for over a month.

FINDING ANYA is a standalone romance novel which is also one of the three books belonging to the Wadhwa siblings. This kindle book remained in #1 Bestseller position on Amazon India for four months from its release.

Even as a child, Sundari absolutely loved the 'lived happily ever after' syndrome and she grew up on a steady diet of fairy tales, Phantom comics and Mandrake comics. It was always about good triumphing over evil and a happy ending after the protagonists surmounted all unexpected obstacles.

Once she entered her teens, Sundari switched her loyalties from fairy tales to Mills & Boon. While she loved reading both, she kept visualising what would have happened if there were similar situations happening in India; to local heroes and heroines. And of course, the joy of vanquishing the ubiquitous evil villains! Her imagination soared and she happily ensconced herself in a rosy romantic cocoon for many years.

Then came the writing—a true bolt from the blue! And Sundari Venkatraman has never looked back.

Books by Sundari Venkatraman

Standalone novels
The Malhotra Bride
Meghna
The Madras Affair
An Autograph for Anjali
Twin Torment
Finding Anya
Mr. Perfect
Man Friday
Her Prince Charming
Love in Agartha
Arjun's Penance
The Floundering Author
Ryan Finds a Bride
Tinder Loving Care
Shaan Gets Hitched
For Better or For Worse
Love… No Conditions Asked

Collection of shorts
Matches Made in Heaven
Tales of Sunshine

Marriages Made in India Series
#1 The Runaway Bridegroom
#2 Her Smitten Husband
#3 His Drunken Wife
#4 Her Secret Husband
#5 The Casanova's Wife
#6 Her Bohemian Husband

The Bansal Legacy Trilogy
#1 Simha International
#2 Rose Garden International
#3 Maharaja International

The Thakore Royals Trilogy
#1 The Marriage Predicament
#2 Tied in Knots
#3 The Wooing of the Shrew

The Groom Series Trilogy
#1 Groomnapped
#2 Gobsmacked
#3 Grounded

Written in the Stars Series
#1 Scorpio Superstar
#2 Leo's Desire
#3 Taurus Temptation
#4 Virgo's Krush
#5 Libra's Flame

Arora Iyers Trilogy
#1 Once Bitten Twice Lucky
#2 Heartthrob
#3 Call of the Heart

Dashavatar (Indian Mythology)
MATSYA: The First Avatar
KURMA: The Second Avatar
VARAHA: The Third Avatar
NARASIMHA: The Fourth Avatar
VAMANA: The Fifth Avatar
PARASHURAMA: The Sixth Avatar

The Princess Series (Historical Romance)
#1 The Passionate Princess
#2 The Rebel Princess

The Writer's Toolkit (Non-fiction)
Publishing Your Book on Amazon KDP

Bollywood Bros Trilogy
#1 Sing For Me
#2 Dance With Me

Romantic Shorts Series
#1 Chahti Hoon Tumhe
#2 Beauty is but Skin Deep
#3 Madeinheaven.com
#4 An Arranged Match
#5 The Reluctant Bride
#6 Shweta ka Swayamvar
#7 Pappa's Girl
#8 Red Rose Dating Agency
#9 Rahat Mili
#10 Reema's Matchmakers
#11 The Matchmaker's Dream

ABOUT THE AUTHOR

Sundari Venkatraman is an Indie Author who has 64 books to her credit. These books have consistently featured in the Top 100 Bestseller Lists on Amazon Kindle, in both romance as well as Asian Drama categories. Her latest hot romances have all been on #1 Bestseller slot in Amazon India for over a month.

FINDING ANYA is a standalone romance novel which is also one of the three books belonging to the Wadhwa siblings. This kindle book remained in #1 Bestseller position on Amazon India for four months from its release.

Even as a child, Sundari absolutely loved the 'lived happily ever after' syndrome and she grew up on a steady diet of fairy tales, Phantom comics and Mandrake comics. It was always about good triumphing over evil and a happy ending after the protagonists surmounted all unexpected obstacles.

Once she entered her teens, Sundari switched her loyalties from fairy tales to Mills & Boon. While she loved reading both, she kept visualising what would have happened if there were similar situations happening in India; to local heroes and heroines. And of course, the joy of vanquishing the ubiquitous evil villains! Her imagination soared and she happily ensconced herself in a rosy romantic cocoon for many years.

Then came the writing—a true bolt from the blue! And Sundari Venkatraman has never looked back.

Books by Sundari Venkatraman

Standalone novels
The Malhotra Bride
Meghna
The Madras Affair
An Autograph for Anjali
Twin Torment
Finding Anya
Mr. Perfect
Man Friday
Her Prince Charming
Love in Agartha
Arjun's Penance
The Floundering Author
Ryan Finds a Bride
Tinder Loving Care
Shaan Gets Hitched
For Better or For Worse
Love… No Conditions Asked

Collection of shorts
Matches Made in Heaven
Tales of Sunshine

Marriages Made in India Series
#1 The Runaway Bridegroom
#2 Her Smitten Husband
#3 His Drunken Wife
#4 Her Secret Husband
#5 The Casanova's Wife
#6 Her Bohemian Husband

The Bansal Legacy Trilogy
#1 Simha International
#2 Rose Garden International
#3 Maharaja International

The Thakore Royals Trilogy
#1 The Marriage Predicament
#2 Tied in Knots
#3 The Wooing of the Shrew

The Groom Series Trilogy
#1 Groomnapped
#2 Gobsmacked
#3 Grounded

Written in the Stars Series
#1 Scorpio Superstar
#2 Leo's Desire
#3 Taurus Temptation
#4 Virgo's Krush
#5 Libra's Flame

Arora Iyers Trilogy
#1 Once Bitten Twice Lucky
#2 Heartthrob
#3 Call of the Heart

Dashavatar (Indian Mythology)
MATSYA: The First Avatar
KURMA: The Second Avatar
VARAHA: The Third Avatar
NARASIMHA: The Fourth Avatar
VAMANA: The Fifth Avatar
PARASHURAMA: The Sixth Avatar

The Princess Series (Historical Romance)
#1 The Passionate Princess
#2 The Rebel Princess

The Writer's Toolkit (Non-fiction)
Publishing Your Book on Amazon KDP

Bollywood Bros Trilogy
#1 Sing For Me
#2 Dance With Me

Romantic Shorts Series
#1 Chahti Hoon Tumhe
#2 Beauty is but Skin Deep
#3 Madeinheaven.com
#4 An Arranged Match
#5 The Reluctant Bride
#6 Shweta ka Swayamvar
#7 Pappa's Girl
#8 Red Rose Dating Agency
#9 Rahat Mili
#10 Reema's Matchmakers
#11 The Matchmaker's Dream

FINDING Anya

(Wadhwas)

A romance novel by

SUNDARI VENKATRAMAN

FLAMING SUN

ISBN 979-8-89066-936-0

Beta Read by: Rubina Ramesh
Edited by: The Book Club Editorial Panel
Cover Illustration: Unaiza Merchant

nya and Farhan Merchant stepped out of the family court in Bandra on Friday, just before noon, grinning widely at each other. Anya turned to hug Farhan, pressing her lips to his cheek. "Thank you so much Farhan. You are my bestest friend."

Farhan hugged her back with equal enthusiasm. "Thank *you*, Anya. I don't really know how I'd have survived the last two years without you."

Anya moved away to look up at her ex-husband, shaking her head. "I'm sure you'd have managed, especially with Arth by your side."

"Oh yes, Arth of course. I can conquer the world along with him. But I hadn't met him then, when my parents were pressurising me to get married. You saved the day."

"Parents!" Anya grimaced, thinking of hers. They had come after her with a stick the moment she had completed her MBA with flying colours. That she was barely twenty-two had not seemed to matter to them. Amal and Gaurav Chhabria had been adamant and of one mind to see their only child married off as soon as possible. The uncles and aunts from the joint family had been no help either, taking her parents' side. They had even looked at a couple of alliances. But luckily, neither had worked. But they had not let off the pressure. And that was how she had ending up marrying Farhan Merchant, her best friend, from the first time they met at play school, all the way to completing their graduation together from the same college. Anya had put her foot down when her parents tried to object to their tying the knot in the name of religion. In the end, they had accepted Farhan as their son-in-law, glad that their daughter was ready to get married, after all.

"Why the heck do they give birth to kids?!" Anya exclaimed with more irritation than anger.

Farhan gave her a pained look. He put out a hand to shake hers. "Well then, I'll be seeing you around Anya. Do be in touch."

She shook hands with the man who had been her husband—only on paper—for almost two years, the one she had divorced barely half an hour ago. "Try and stop me," she grinned. "And thanks for the use of the apartment."

Farhan shook his head again. "Not just for use, Anya. It's yours to keep."

Yes, Farhan had a big heart. He had transferred the two-bedroom-hall-kitchen apartment where they had lived, to Anya's name, despite her protests. Well, just now it was a place to stay. But Anya had no intention of taking advantage of her best friend. He had bought it with his hard-earned money and it was not as if he owed her alimony. Their divorce had been by mutual consent, same as their marriage, two friends helping each other out in a time of trouble.

She shrugged, looking at him. "Oh by the way, don't forget. Not a word to my parents of our divorce. I don't want them sweeping back into my life. I've just got my freedom and…"

"Oh, you've been feeling tied down with me since our marriage," winked Farhan, a mischievous look on his face.

"Hahaha! Of course not. But you know what I mean about being absolutely free and independent."

Farhan nodded. "The same goes to my parents too. Though I don't think they will get in touch with you." His parents were reclusive and had washed their hands off their elder son after he got married to a girl who did not belong to their Parsi community.

"Sure," said Anya. "I'll see you then." With a smile and a wave, Anya walked away from him. She was free! Free to live her life exactly the way she wanted. She did her best to keep her face straight, lowering her eyes so that she would not be mistaken for a crazy woman, laughing all by herself. She went to the parking area and got into her car, sitting in it for a few minutes to absorb her jubilation. She had never been so happy in all of her twenty-four years. Looking into the rear-view mirror, she saw her dark brown eyes glowing. She ran her fingers through her thick, curly hair, pushing at the locks which tended to fall on her forehead. Free! Free! Free!

Anya drove out of the parking lot, her mind on reflex mode as she mentally made a list of all the things which she needed to complete that day. She had taken the day off from work and the long weekend stretched luxuriously in front of her. It had been big of Farhan to write over his flat to her. Considering that it was in an excellent locality in Bandra, not far from the sea, she was lucky indeed. She had never expected that. The slow-moving traffic failed to bother her as she sang along with the music blaring from her car radio, a smile not far from her lips.

Horns tooted behind her when the signal turned green. Right at the front of the line, Anya shifted her white Audi into first gear before moving forward, not noticing the speeding truck that had broken the signal on the opposite side and was swooping towards her.

Anya did not know what hit her as she felt her body being lifted up in the air before it fell down with a thud, her ears protesting the noise of the screech of metal against metal before the world turned black, shutting everything out.

Farhan waved off Anya before taking out his cell to call his boyfriend, Arth Sharma. "Hey," called out Farhan, a smile in his voice, confident of being loved. "It's gone through, my divorce. I've the papers with me."

"Awesome," replied Arth, equally enthusiastic. "You've taken the whole day off, right? Why don't you come over to my shop? Let's celebrate."

"Done. On my way," said Farhan, walking towards the car park. He got into his car, chatting away to Arth as he reversed. "See you then. I'm disconnecting my phone as I'm driving towards the gate."

"See you," said Arth.

Farhan drove out of the gates, speeding as he was in a hurry to reach his lover. This was the first time he was going to meet Arth as a free man. Just as he moved towards the signal, he saw that a lorry had crashed into a car. The car was completely crushed and unrecognisable. Wondering if he should stop to help, he heard a police siren along with an ambulance. He also noticed a tall man standing there, guiding the traffic, obviously having taken charge of the scene. Pushing away his guilt, Farhan roared away from there, eager to get to Vashi, unaware that it was his ex-wife and best friend who had met with an accident.

Dev Wadhwa stood there, near the crushed car, guiding the traffic along with a police constable. He had been waiting at the opposite signal in his steel grey Innova Crysta, third in line behind the truck. Seeing the accident happen right there in front of him, Dev had jumped out of his car to rush to the spot. The truck driver would not have stopped if Dev had not yelled out to him, taking pictures of both the driver and the licence plate with his iPhone. As for the car, it was crushed almost flat, beyond recognition.

It was a woman driver and she had been thrown clean out, cracking her head against the divider. Dev walked over to her to find out what state she was in and turned pale under his tan when he saw who it was.

Anya!

Oh my God! He had not foreseen their meeting to be under such terrible circumstances after all these years. Not that he had ever expected to meet her.

Pushing away the thoughts swirling in this mind, Dev reached out a trembling hand to touch the pulse at her throat and breathed a sigh of relief when he found it fluttering under his finger. Taking a deep breath to calm himself, Dev straightened to take his phone out once again. He called an ambulance service as well as the police, in that order. Luckily, there was no fire, but he could not get to either Anya's cell phone or any identification as the car was totally mangled.

While he remembered her first name, he could not recall the surname and did not know whom to contact. Her things were obviously stuck inside the crushed car and were not accessible. He had no choice but to wait for help.

The traffic cop arrived on the scene, soon after Dev finished with his calls. When asked, the cop whined about having gone to the public toilet which was a distance away, on a side road. Well—Dev mentally shrugged to himself—that was that, no apology given.

Before the ambulance arrived, Dev had called a mechanic friend of his, requesting him to take his car away. There was no way that Dev was going to leave Anya alone during her ride to the hospital.

The ambulance arrived along with the police. "Lady driver. No wonder there was an accident," declared the police inspector, a sarcastic smile on his face.

Dev gritted his teeth, holding back his temper. "No Inspector. The lady was driving correctly in this case. She started her car when the signal turned green, in fact, only after the cars behind her started honking. But the truck driver drove fast, *after* the signal turned red. He was at fault."

"And how would you know?" asked the inspector, a scowl on his face. He wanted to wrap the case up as fast and as easily as possible. If the victim was at fault, there was bound to be less trouble.

"I was at the opposite signal…"

"I think you should be on your way, mister. You couldn't have seen much from so far away." The policeman smirked, feeling all powerful.

Dev gave the other man an intimidating look from his dark grey eyes, visibly shaking the man up. "I definitely saw way more from the other side than what you could see from your police station, *sir*." Sarcasm dripped from his voice. "I was one car behind the truck and had stopped as the signal turned red. The truck did not. The woman in the car started hers because the vehicles behind her were impatient to leave as their signal had turned green. Anyway, the ambulance is here and I'll need to go with the victim. Do you want to take my name and contact number, just in case?" Dev turned as if to go, impatience in every line of his body.

"Wait a minute, who the hell are you to take charge? I'm the police here," the inspector snarled, his ego refusing to take a beating.

"I agree. And you have a lot of work to do here as the car is smashed beyond recognition. And the truck driver is sitting across in his vehicle, refusing to co-operate. We don't have an identity on the victim and I couldn't find either her cell phone or her purse or whatever she was carrying. I couldn't even see the license plate. There's no way of contacting her family…"

"You're going too fast, young man. Let the law do its work."

"Of course, sir. I'll be on my way then," said Dev. He had noticed that Anya had been settled inside the ambulance and was keen to leave with her.

"Stop right here; give me your name and number. And show me your identification too," said the inspector belligerently, not liking the idea of being thwarted.

Dev bit his lip to stop himself from smiling despite his anxiety, handing his driving license to the inspector. He also took out a small notebook he carried in his pocket, wrote his name and phone number and tearing out the page, handed it to the constable hovering behind the inspector. Taking his license from the inspector's hand, he sprinted across to the ambulance, impatient to get the unconscious Anya to a doctor. He instructed the ambulance driver to take them to Leelavati Hospital which was not very far away.

Dev sat beside the prone figure of Anya, his heart bleeding for her. He touched her forehead, gently pushing back the few strands of hair which had fallen over it. Not surprisingly, her face was extraordinarily pale. He held her slender wrist between his thumb and forefinger to check her pulse. He found to his relief that it was still beating, though on the erratic side. Dev took her hand in both of his, holding it between his palms, saying a silent prayer that she recovered quickly. He could not help but notice the contrast between their hands. Hers was small and white as it lay in his large, tanned hands. Without realising what he was doing, Dev raised her hand and pressed his lips to the centre of her palm, his heart going out to her, willing her to become alright. He could not help recalling… no, he had better not go there, not now, when he needed all his wits about him to get Anya back on her feet.

The ambulance reached the hospital within ten minutes and stopped at the entrance to the emergency ward. Luckily, Dev had contacts there. Anya was taken in without too many questions asked. She needed urgent treatment and she was going to get it.

Dr. Adnani stepped out after half an hour to talk to Dev. "While the good news is that no other part of her body is injured, the victim has cracked her head when it hit the pavement. There's internal bleeding is what I see from preliminary tests. There will be more tests to be conducted. I'd like to know upfront who will foot the bills. Would you know if she has medical insurance? You do understand that…"

"No worries, Dr. Adnani. I'll handle all that. In fact, I can pay in advance if necessary. You can bill it to my company's account as I know only the first name of the victim."

Dr. Adnani turned around to call out to a nurse. "Guide Mr. Wadhwa to the billing counter, and before you go…" He turned to a station to pick up the hospital's prescription pad to scribble some instructions on it quickly. Handing it over to the nurse, he said, "These are the tests and immediate treatments for the accident victim. Get a bill made in the name of this gentleman's company." The doctor nodded to Dev. "You can go along with Nurse Saldana, Mr. Wadhwa. And thank you. That's truly a weight off my mind. And oh, by the way, have the police been notified?"

Dev nodded. "Of course, doctor. They are working on finding Anya's identification even as we talk." He surreptitiously crossed his fingers behind his back. The police inspector did not seem to give a damn about anything. He wondered if they might have got anywhere with the investigation. Well, Dev was his own boss and had all the time in the world. It was just that he was worried for Anya's family. They must surely be perturbed that she had not reached home or wherever she had been going.

He went along with Nurse Saldana to pay the bills. "Wadhwa Farm is the name of my company. Please bill it in that name." He removed a visiting card and handed it over to the man in charge of accounts.

Dev went to sit on a visitor's chair, making a few urgent calls while the accountant got all the requisite forms together. After filling the multiple forms and completing the rest of the formalities, he asked for the way to the canteen to get himself a cup of much-needed coffee.

I t was a little more than two days since the accident. Anya was in a coma and Dr. Adnani could not tell Dev when she might be out of it, if at all. But there was no way that Dev was going to leave Anya by herself. He booked a suite at the hospital and stayed there along with her, working out of the hospital room, using his mobile and laptop to carry out his business dealings. He had instructed Shaan, his assistant, to manage the farm. There were many orders to be fulfilled, but he was confident that Shaan would be able to handle them all.

Dev was also constantly in touch with the police. He had even visited the police station twice to find out if they had any information. Anya's mobile was in smithereens and was of no help. They had not been able to find a handbag either. Dev wanted to scream in frustration. He was sure that someone had stolen her purse or handbag, whatever she had been carrying. How could someone drive a car without anything? For all he knew, it could be someone from the police department who had flicked it. "But sir, there must have been some kind of paper in the vehicle, right? Please give me the license number. I'll try to trace the owner myself."

Police Inspector Borkar smirked. "What's the hurry, Wadhwa? We are all so busy here, working on so many cases. Only yesterday, there was a bomb scare in a school. And today morning…" He droned on and on about the importance of police work.

A visibly annoyed Dev wished the man a 'good day' and left the police station, frustration in every line of his body. He had been tracking the news on TV channels as well as newspapers in case her face had been splashed as a missing person. No use asking the police for help regarding the same as they were so non-cooperative.

A deep sigh shook him from the core of his being. A few years back, Anya's relatives had been his parents' neighbours. They had moved away subsequently. Dev had even called his estranged mother to get a contact number. But it looked like the Madhvanis had not left an address or contact number.

Dev was not too social media savvy though he had a Facebook account. He opened it now to check for Anya. Clicking on people under the name Anya, he scrolled and then he scrolled some more—down the page to see so many accounts, some Indian and many foreign ones. Damn it! It was like looking for a needle in a haystack. A random search across Google as well as Google images yielded nothing. He hesitantly opened his LinkedIn account, only to find so many Anyas there too. But there was none with curly shoulder length hair, wheat complexion, a tip-tilted nose and coffee brown eyes which fitted the woman who was lying in a coma.

Giving up after a while, Dev walked up and down the hospital room, wondering how to deal with the problem. As he turned to look at Anya, he could not help but feel sorry for her. If he remembered right, she would be about twenty-four years old. Her parents must be worried crazy, wondering what must have happened to her. They lived somewhere in Punjab, in Chandigarh if he was not mistaken. And Anya, he did not really know if she lived with them or here in Mumbai. Could she have taken up a job somewhere? In that case, wouldn't her colleagues miss her? Was it so easy for a person to disappear in Mumbai? Damn it! She had been driving a car. There was her license, her car number plate and so many other things which could help them trace her family. Why the hell was no one bothered?

Dev turned around in a hurry when he thought he heard a groan of pain, startled to see that Anya's eyes were open in a slit, as she looked vaguely in his direction. He walked close to the bed, a wide smile on his face. Thank God for that! Now he did not need the police's help to trace her parents.

She woke up in the hospital, alone—or so she thought—not noticing the man who was burning a hole in the carpet with his pacing. Her head was throbbing in pain and she could open her eyes barely a slit as she took in her surroundings. She raised a hand to her head or at least tried to. There were needles stuck in her arm, connected to tubes and monitors. She turned her head with great difficulty as a groan inadvertently broke out from her throat. She tried to talk, but no sound came. Had she lost her voice?

"Hello," said Dev softly, not wanting to startle her. While he had immediately recognised Anya, Dev wondered if she would remember him. He watched as her eyes opened wider, feeling the strong pull of attraction as he looked deeply into her chocolate brown eyes. She was even more beautiful than before.

"Who are you?" Her voice was a croak.

Anya did not remember him. Though he did not want to attach too much importance to it, Dev could not help feeling rather shaken by the fact. Pushing his thoughts away, he rang the bell for the nurse before pouring some water into a glass and letting her sip from it, giving her time to swallow. "I am Dev."

She nodded before groaning again. "My head's hurting, terribly. What happened to me?"

Nurse Saldana walked in, calling out a cheerful, "Good evening, ma'am. Lovely to see you awake." She took her patient's wrist to check her pulse and found it a bit erratic even now. "Dr. Adnani should be coming in fifteen minutes during his rounds. Now tell me, what's your full name?" she asked.

She stared at the nurse, bewilderment on her face. "Name?" A heavy scowl marred her forehead as she thought hard, delving into the depths of her mind to find an answer, before an expression of horror overtook her lovely face. "I don't know," she said in a whisper.

The shocked nurse gave Dev a startled glance before patting the patient's shoulder awkwardly. "Let me go get the doctor."

It was Sunday evening when Amal Chhabria lost it with her daughter. "Irresponsible girl! I have been trying to reach her since yesterday morning and look at her, she has switched off her phone. I know she is busy the whole week. But can she not speak to her parents at least during the weekend?" Amal continued to complain to her husband Gaurav who was watching the cricket match with total concentration. "*Kyunji*, did you listen to even one word I said? This is how it has always been. Only the mother should worry all the time. The father never cares." Her voice had been rising by a few decibels with each sentence.

Without removing his eyes from the TV screen, Gaurav replied, "I'm sure our neighbours also heard you, Amal. And why should I worry? You do that enough for half a dozen people, all by yourself. If you can't get in touch with Anya, why don't you call Farhan? Her phone is probably broken for all you know and she needs to buy a new one." Gaurav did not understand the need to fret for every small thing.

Amal made a face at her husband before dialling Anya's husband's number. "Hello Farhan, how are you?" she gushed. She was ever so grateful to the boy for marrying her daughter and giving her a life. Otherwise, the girl would still be at her mother's house, eating her head. What all trouble had Amal undergone to bring up her tomboy of a daughter?!

"I'm good, Amal Aunty. How are you and Gaurav Uncle?" asked Farhan warmly, even as he wondered furiously about why Anya's mother had called him.

"We both are fine, *beta*. Where is Anya? I've been calling her since yesterday. Is her phone not working?"

Farhan thought on his feet. He remembered Anya's instructions only too well, not to let on to her parents that they were divorced. "Aunty, Anya has gone out with her friends. Let me try to find out if I can contact one of them."

"What? She has gone out with her friends, leaving you at home? How can you allow that, Farhan? Has she no respect for you, her husband?" Amal was shocked at her daughter's behaviour. Yes, more than usual. "You get her to call me and I'll definitely give her a piece of my mind."

Farhan frowned, wondering what kind of trouble he was getting Anya into. Her mother was Hitler personified. She would go to any lengths in the name of culture and tradition. "*Nahi* Aunty. It's nothing like that. I had to go to a bachelor's party and so..."

Amal laughed. "Oh, like that! Then it's fine." Yes, if the man needed time by himself, then the woman should undoubtedly adjust. "Okay then. You get her to call me, will you? And don't forget to tell her that I'm annoyed with her," said Amal, before disconnecting the phone.

So, what was new? Farhan thought. This was exactly the problem Anya had faced throughout her life—a disapproving mother, an indifferent father and a few other nosy relatives living together in a joint family. No wonder she valued her freedom. He remembered Anya mentioning that she wanted to spend time by herself at the flat, reading, and relaxing. He speed-dialled her number to find that it was switched off. He went to the kitchen to find his partner making coffee. "Arth, do you want to go for a ride? I need to go to Anya's apartment for a visit."

Arth turned to look at Farhan. "Is there a problem?" he asked, handing the other man a mug.

"Her phone is switched off and her mother has been trying to reach her over the last few days. I don't know, but something is niggling at me."

Arth said, "Let's go then," and finished his coffee in a few gulps.

It did not take them long to reach Anya's apartment building in Bandra, as there was not much traffic on the Sunday evening. The security guard greeted Farhan. "*Salaam saab!*"

Farhan smiled and waved at him as he drove further down to the car park. Anya's car was not there in the place allotted for it. Sighing, he decided to go up to her flat anyway, with Arth at his side. She had given the car for service, maybe.

Farhan rang the bell of flat 704 a couple of times. After waiting for a few minutes, he took the key he still had with him to open the apartment. Silence greeted them as the two men entered the precincts.

The apartment looked empty. Farhan walked around, checking things, wondering about Anya's whereabouts, while Arth opened the balcony door, letting in some fresh air. Farhan stepped into the kitchen to find two coffee cups. But… if he remembered right, they were the cups from the time he had had coffee with Anya on Friday morning. Did that mean she had never returned to the flat after leaving the family court at Bandra? He clearly remembered her telling him that she was going home first.

"Arth," Farhan's voice was extremely disturbed. "Something is definitely wrong. Anya did not get back home from court that day."

"And how do you know?" asked Arth, looking at his partner keenly.

Farhan took him to the kitchen to show him the coffee cups. "I had coffee with her before we left for the court. She did not come home. Wait a minute… oh my God! Arth!" Farhan sat down suddenly, holding his head in his hands. "Please God, let it not be so," he groaned, his voice breaking.

Arth sat next to Farhan, hugging him tight. "What is it, Farhan? What did you remember?"

Farhan turned tortured eyes to Arth. "There had been a terrible accident at the signal when I left the family court that day. It was…"

"But you left at the same time as Anya did, right?" asked Arth, hoping against hope that Farhan was wrong.

Farhan shook his head. "No, she left a few minutes ahead of me. You remember I spoke to you after getting the divorce cleared?" Arth nodded, encouraging him to go on. "Anya had left before I called you. I left a few minutes later and saw a major accident at the signal. I didn't stop when I noticed that someone was already handling the matter. I..." Farhan broke down, completely.

Arth held him close, rubbing his back, not uttering a word. When Farhan calmed down after a few minutes, Arth said, "Don't presume the worst. Let's call a few of her friends and colleagues, just in case."

Farhan nodded, quickly running through the list of common friends he had with his ex-wife. Nobody had heard from her. There was one more person's number he had—an office colleague of Anya's, named Sheetal. Farhan dialled her number, holding Arth's arm in a death grip. Sheetal picked up on the seventh ring.

"Hi Sheetal, I need to know something urgently. Has Anya been in touch with you?"

"No Farhan. Why, is something the matter? Anya had taken the Friday off. She mentioned it was an urgent family matter. Then with the weekend looming, we haven't been in touch. But then, you'd know more about her whereabouts, right? Being her husband and all that." Sheetal laughed at her own weak joke.

Farhan shook his head negatively at Arth before saying 'bye' to Sheetal and disconnecting the phone. "Should we go to the police?" he asked Arth pathetically.

"Better yet, let's go meet my father. He knows the Police Commissioner personally."

The two men shut Anya's apartment swiftly before going down the lift. Farhan stopped the car on their way out to talk to the security guard. "Anya madam *kho dekha kya?*" he asked through the window.

"*Nahi saab.* She went with you two days ago in the morning, right? She hasn't come back after that."

Farhan nodded his head, thanking the man, before driving away with a screech of his tyres.

Dr. Adnani ordered both MRI and CT scans for the morning, before he sat down with his patient to conduct an AMI test. The Autobiographical Memory Interview is a set of questions that a doctor creates to fit every patient, trying to find out the level of the patient's recall of their life before the accident.

Anya's bed had been raised by forty-five degrees so that she could comfortably face the doctor. Well, the comfort was only in her position as a sheen of tears shone in her chocolate brown eyes, even as her lips trembled in anxiety.

Dr. Adnani put on his best bedside manner as he spoke to her. "Well, ma'am, I'd like to ask you a few questions. Let me tell you upfront that I am recording this Q & A session as it might help me find something useful at a later point, even if I have missed it during the session. Are you able to understand me?"

"Yes, doctor," said Anya in a broken voice.

"So, let's start with a few simple questions. Nothing that you need to worry about. Just relax and tell me what you know. What is your name?"

A tear rolled down her left cheek as she shook her head slightly, putting her hands up to hold her head in reflex as it hurt badly. "I don't know."

"Hmm. Are you a student?"

"I don't know." Another tear followed the first.

"Or maybe you go to work. Okay, what is your line of interest?"

"I don't know." She lifted a hand to wipe her face with the tissue from the box Nurse Saldana had left on the table next to her bed.

"Do you play chess?"

She paused, thinking. "Is it a game?"

So, she could connect 'play' with 'game'. The doctor felt a bit relieved. "Yes. Do you play the game?"

"I don't know."

"Are you from Mumbai?"

"You mean the Island City? I don't know, doctor."

So, she could connect that Mumbai was also the Island City. Hope filled the doctor as he asked her many more questions on similar lines, moving from personal to impersonal in sudden spurts. At the end of it, he concluded that she had absolutely no memory of her personal life until the time she woke up in the hospital room. But she could connect to general information.

Dr. Adnani finished with the interview and called Dev Wadhwa over to his consulting room to speak to him in private.

She stared up at the ceiling, her mind totally blank. It felt as if her brain had been replaced with cotton wool. She thought and she thought, but nothing came into her mind. Not a single thing other than the nurse, the doctor and the man who had introduced himself as Dev, who obviously did not belong to the hospital staff. He was friendly and nice. She did not feel threatened by his presence. Now why did that thought come? Did she feel threatened by the presence of other people? She scowled at the ceiling. Who was Dev? And how did he know her? He told her that her name was Anya. But if that was her name, shouldn't she feel some kind of connection to it? Only she felt nothing.

Then again, he only knew her first name and not her surname. They could not find her parents or any other person who knew her. But then, how did Dev know her name? Did they know each other? She—okay, Anya—was confused.

Dr. Adnani had asked her a lot of questions. Their session had run to almost an hour. While she could grasp some of the things he was talking about, she had no answers to give him about herself. Her life until yesterday was a blank canvas. Would she ever remember? She had asked the doctor that. While he had reassured her a lot, he did not have a direct answer to that question.

She had asked for a mirror, but had kept it aside when the nurse had brought it to her, afraid of what she might find. Well, she had wanted to be alone when she looked inside it. Thinking that now was a good time, she took the hand mirror which was fairly big and held it in front of her face. A stranger's reflection stared back at her. She studied the face minutely, searching for something, anything which she could recognise. Her face was oval and pale. Thick, dark, and curly hair framed her face, with bangs that insisted on falling on her wide forehead. Her black eyebrows were shapely. Her eyes were the colour of coffee, framed by luxuriant, curly lashes, as they stared at her blankly with no recognition in them. Her cheeks were thin, separated by a tip-tilted nose, while her lips were pink and generous, especially the lower one. But who was she? No clue.

Anya could see her face turning even paler than before as she stared at her reflection in the mirror. Who was she? What did she do? Where did she live? Who were her parents? Was she married? Did she have a boyfriend? A dry sob tore from her throat as Anya bit her nails in anxiety, throwing the mirror face down on the bed. She did not know a damn thing.

Anya's breath came in gasps as she beat herself up mentally. How could she not remember? Come on, she was an adult. What had happened to her all these years? The doctor had guessed that she must be in her twenties. She wondered if she was still in college or if she worked somewhere. Her parents must be wondering what had happened to her. Weren't they out there looking for her? Did she have siblings? Nothing clicked. Not one single answer. All that thinking gave her a pounding headache, making her want to throw up. Where was Dev? She needed him by her side. His presence gave her at least a modicum of peace.

In the meanwhile, Dev was sitting with Dr. Adnani as the latter explained Anya's condition to him. "The human brain is such an amazing as well as a delicate organ. Anya's accident has resulted in her suffering from Traumatic Amnesia. Amnesia is when a person forgets a section of their personal life incidents. When that happens because of an accident, it is called Traumatic Amnesia. Only time will tell if it is Retrograde Amnesia. When a patient suffers from this, it means they have forgotten only their past, but will be able to form new memories. Well, the young lady remembered your name when I asked her about you. She told me she knew you were Dev Wadhwa because you had told her that that was your name. Which gives us hope as it appears that she's able to retain new information." The doctor paused, looking at the young man in front of him. "Are you able to absorb what I am telling you or am I going too fast?"

Dev replied, "I've read a bit about amnesia, though the medical terms are new to me. It's just that I'm wondering how to deal with this. The police haven't been able to trace Anya's identity. What are the chances of her recovering her memory once her wound is healed? And how long do you think that might take?"

The doctor sighed. "I'm truly sorry to say that I can't tell you anything about her regaining her memory. The wound is healing well and she should be on her feet in a few days. After that, she just needs to take care that she doesn't strain herself too much for a couple of months. Physically, she's absolutely fit. I also had a few tests conducted that all the parts and organs of her body are functioning normally. But we cannot predict when or even *if* she will ever regain her memory. This is a tricky situation and medicine has no solution to this."

Dev stared at the doctor, trying to absorb the magnitude of what the older man was telling him.

That meant she would not be able to get back with her family. He got up to shake the doctor's hand. "When will be a good time to discharge Anya?" he asked.

"Let me see. Today is Sunday. I think another four days to go. Maybe Thursday or Friday?"

Dev nodded. "Thank you for your time, doctor." He smiled. "You must be overworked surely. Do you work all seven days of the week?" he asked.

Dr. Adnani smiled. "Overworked, yes. But I do take a weekly off. We can't leave the hospital unattended, so there's a skeleton staff working on Sundays too."

Dev left the consultation room to go directly to the hospital room. Anya would need a lot of cheering up. The doctor had mentioned chess and Dev had had someone buy a set and deliver it at the hospital reception. He planned to play a couple of rounds with her after dinner, if she was willing.

Anya's sad face lightened up when she caught sight of Dev. "Hello, did you get to meet the doctor?"

Dev nodded. "Yes."

"What did he say? When will I remember? I'm an adult and I don't know a damn thing about myself. I don't even know where I live. Do you?" Her face crumpled.

Dev walked to the bed and placed an arm around her slim shoulders, pulling her head to his chest. He rubbed a large hand soothingly down her back. "I know, sweetheart." He pressed his lips to the top of her head, careful of the stitches at the back. "Will you let me be your friend? You can come to live with me if we are unable to find your address. I have a big house in Karjat and live there with my grandmother."

She looked up at him with her melting brown eyes. "Won't I be intruding upon your life?"

He shook his head. "Not at all. *Chalo*, let's have dinner. I'll order Chinese food from a restaurant. Do you like Chinese cuisine?" he asked, looking at her keenly.

"Noodles and chicken gravy?" she asked, her eyes lighting up. "Oh, yum."

So, it was her personal memories which had disappeared, as the doctor had mentioned. Dev nodded at her with a smile. "Yes, that's what I'll ask for."

"And Dev, how come you know my name? Do we know each other?" she asked, a frown on her forehead.

"Not very well. But we have met." What else to tell her? It was the truth anyway. Okay, a little less than the truth. But what use would it be telling her that they had been on a date once and even shared a brief kiss on a terrace under the moonlight? And how could he tell her that he had run away scared by the passion she had invoked in him? He had been barely twenty-five, five years ago and not at all ready for commitment. He had been attracted to her and had just wanted to have fun. But he had been totally unprepared for the brush of her soft lips against his mouth which had been like a powerful kick to his solar plexus. And yes, he had run away from the spot, even more shaken by the hurt expression on her face. And it had haunted him forever.

Dev left Anya by herself in the hospital room, to go down and collect their dinner and chess set from the reception. While he did his best to draw her into a conversation, Anya kept going silent as she ate her dinner. He was happy to note that she seemed to relish the food, at least. And when he opened the topic of books, she turned animated, talking about many authors, bringing him hope.

Anya gave a squeal of delight when Dev set up the chess board. "I love this game." She beat him on all three rounds that they played before Nurse Saldana came in with her night medication.

Once the nurse left, Anya asked Dev in a small voice, "You'll not leave me here alone, will you?" Fear clouded her eyes as they stared at him.

He shook his head. "No, I won't, sweetheart. You see the bed at the other end?" When she nodded, he said, "That is where I'll be sleeping. Don't hesitate to call me if you need anything."

She gave him a small nod. "Will you give me a hug?" She felt so safe in his arms, held against his large, warm body.

He walked to her bed and lay down next to her, holding her against his chest. "Go to sleep, sweetheart. I promise not to go away."

And she slept, the medicines taking effect quickly as she was tired out from all the trauma of waking up after the accident. He got up after he sensed that her breathing had evened out in sleep, although he felt reluctant to leave her side.

Dev lay on his bed, staring up at the hospital room ceiling, his eyes not really focused as his mind went back five years.

6

There were still three months to go before Dev turned twenty-five when he returned from the USA after completing his MBA at the University of Georgia. He was planning his farm, getting all the documents and licenses together, while fighting an ongoing battle with his parents, Karishma and Durgesh Wadhwa. Both his parents were corporate slaves. It was after looking at their hectic lives that Dev became absolutely sure that he was not going to become one. Dev knew his mind and was clear about his goals.

When he broached the subject of farming, his father's first reaction was, "Are you mad, Dev? You went all the way to the United States only to return and become a farmer?" Durgesh Wadhwa scowled at his eldest born, his bushy eyebrows meeting in the middle of his forehead. "When you got a full-fledged scholarship, I was so proud and thought you would take up a job there in America. What is there to keep you in India?"

"Why Dad? I enjoy living in India. Two years abroad was a good experience. And yes, I'd like to see more of the world. But I want to live right here, in my home country."

"Karishma, listen to your son," called out Durgesh. "The whole world is progressing while Dev is moving in the reverse," he said with a sarcastic smile.

"Why don't you get a job to suit your qualification, Dev?" asked his mother. "Okay, maybe you want to live in Mumbai. Fair enough. Multinationals will simply grab you if you apply to them." Dev had always been a difficult child. She never could understand him. It was his grandmother Meena Wadhwa that he spent most of his time with. But then, Karishma could not have managed a rocking marketing career and the twins who had just turned eighteen this year, without her mother-in-law's help.

"I have set my heart on this farm, Mom. I'm going with it," said Dev firmly, getting up from the breakfast table. He had too much planned for the day and arguing with his parents was simply getting in the way.

"If you don't change your mind, I'll simply cut you out of my will," threatened Durgesh, his eyes turning red with temper.

"Dad," Dev walked to his father and placed a hand on his shoulder. "I'm planning to be so rich that I'll amass way more than what you can leave me in your will," he said softly. "I'm good as long as you both hold me in your hearts," he smiled.

Durgesh was stumped, not knowing how to react to that. Once Dev stepped out of the dining room, Karishma said, "Let him do what he wants for a year or two. He will probably change his mind once he knows the kind of back-breaking work he will need to do with farming. Let him be for now."

Durgesh nodded reluctantly. What were they going to tell their relatives, friends, and colleagues? They would laugh their heads off if they heard that their son had turned to agriculture after the kind of education he had had *and* after passing out with flying colours.

The duo made it clear at every point that they were ashamed of the choice their son had made, not that it stopped Dev from doing exactly what he wanted. But yes, deep down, he was terribly hurt. Though worse was yet to come.

The Wadhwas lived in a row house in Vashi and shared a common wall with the Madhvanis. That morning, when Dev stepped out of their home to get on his bike, he heard a tinkling laugh. Walking to the compound wall, he saw a young woman gurgling with laughter as she played with the Madhvani kids who were still preteens. She looked about sixteen, her long, curly hair up in a pony. Her laughter was so infectious that it brought a smile to Dev's face. He found her too attractive for words.

"Mom, are the Madhvanis having guests at their home?" Dev asked his mother that night at dinner, "I saw this girl playing with the kids there."

"That must be Anya," said his sister Chaahat. "She's Niti's cousin from Punjab. Anya is nineteen and has just finished her degree. She's taking a break before doing her MBA."

Dev smiled at his sister, delighted to know all the details without having to ask too many questions. Her name was Anya. It suited her. If she was from Punjab, he wondered how long she planned to stay in Mumbai. He had to meet her, but in private; might not be that simple with so many people around, but he was not giving up without trying.

Later at night, his mother said, "I spoke to Sonal Madhvani. I understand that Anya's parents are on the lookout for a husband for her. Do you want Dad to ask for her hand for you?" His parents had concluded that getting him married was a sure-fire way to stop Dev from turning to farming. Which modern woman would want a farmer for her husband?

Dev shrugged, not really paying attention to his mother's words. Marriage was a long-term plan. He had not really thought about it. Taking his shrug as assent, Karishma decided to talk to her husband and take the matter further.

At eleven that night, Dev sat on the second-floor terrace, talking on his phone when he saw Anya on the Madhvanis' terrace. And she was alone. Cutting the call, he waved to her, "Hey!"

She gave him a hesitant smile. She had noticed the handsome hunk a couple of times in the past twenty-four hours since she had arrived at her uncle's home. She also knew that his name was Dev. "Hi!"

Dev climbed over the wall which separated the two terraces and went to meet her, thrilled with the opportunity. She was even more beautiful at close proximity. "I'm Dev."

"Anya," she said, a trifle breathless at finding him this close. She studied him boldly though, taking in his attractive features.

Seeing the book in her hand, he asked, "Do you read a lot?"

She nodded enthusiastically, "Oh yes! I love reading. Do you?"

"I do." They chatted about this and that, while their eyes held a dialogue at a different level. "Would you like to go for a coffee tomorrow?" he asked.

She looked up at him and decided to be upfront. "I don't think my uncle will approve. I don't want him to complain to my parents." She grimaced. "I'm sorry," she apologised.

"Hmm." His grey eyes turned mischievous. "Would you like to meet me somewhere away from Vashi? I can pick you up on my bike at the end of the street. What say?" he asked, his eyebrow up in query.

She studied his face for a few seconds. He was thoroughly likeable and polite to boot. What was the harm? A grin lit her gamine features. "I say yes."

"That's my girl. Does six o'clock work? Can you get away?"

Anya nodded. "I'll manage," she said, smiling into his eyes.

The next evening, Anya sat pillion on Dev's bike, holding on to his well-muscled shoulders, doing her best to keep some space between their bodies. It was such fun, meeting him clandestinely. She had never felt the urge to meet a man on the sly like this, before now. He rode via Palm Beach Road, and on to Kharghar. It was a long ride and Anya relaxed her body, settling against his hard back, her arms locked around his narrow waist.

He stopped the bike outside the Café Coffee Day outlet at Kharghar. "Do you have a curfew?" he asked.

Anya rolled her eyes, smiling at him. "He asks me now."

Dev grinned at her, his grey eyes roving over her attractive features, her hair windblown even as her coffee brown eyes sparkled with excitement. "So?" His brow went up in query.

She stared at him in wonder. He was probably the handsomest man she had ever set eyes on. How come he wanted to spend time with her, Anya from Punjab? "Are you going to get out of buying me the coffee you promised?" she asked, tongue-in-cheek.

Dev threw back his head and laughed, taking her hand in his and walking into the coffee shop. They found a table for two at a corner in the open-air seating area. "What would you like to have?" he asked.

"Chocolate flavoured coffee, if it's no trouble," she said, smiling politely.

"Anything to eat?"

She shook her head.

He placed an order for two cups of *Café Mocha*, returning to their table after paying the bill. They chatted as they waited for their order. "Anya," he said, taking infinite pleasure in saying her name, "Where do you live in Punjab?"

"I was born and brought up in Chandigarh. And you Dev? Have you always lived in Mumbai?"

"Most of my life. I studied in Panchgani, living in a hostel there." Also the reason why he preferred the clean air in the hills to the pollution of Mumbai.

While he was keen to share his farming plans with her, he decided to talk about it after he got to know her some more. His parents' reactions had not exactly been encouraging. And his siblings, Jai and Chaahat, who were a year younger than Anya, believed that the profession he had chosen was pretty uncool.

After barely half an hour into the conversation, Anya said, "I think it's best we leave now, Dev."

He nodded, getting up immediately. As they walked out of the coffee shop, he asked, "So, would you like to go out again tomorrow?"

"Let me see. I don't know if my aunt has planned anything. I'll let you know."

Dev was disappointed. But then, he was too much of a gentleman to pressure a woman into spending time with him. "Sure," he said, handing her a helmet before placing his own firmly on his head. He dropped her at the point he had picked her up, waiting for her to take the turning towards their row houses, before following her on his bike.

What Dev did not know was that his parents had already set the ball rolling for an alliance between him and Anya and had spoken to the Madhvanis regarding the same.

It was more than twenty-four hours after their coffee date and Dev was keen to meet Anya again. And that is how he landed at his terrace the night after. He had been waiting for almost forty-five minutes when she turned up on her uncle's terrace, making Dev's heart go hammering against his chest.

She was gorgeous and he had enjoyed their conversation at the coffee shop. Though their tastes varied, they both liked reading books. Dev hoped that she planned to stay in Mumbai for some time and they could get to know each other a bit more before she took off to complete her MBA and he to building his farm.

With his heart in his throat, Dev jumped over the wall to her side of the terrace and said, "Hey, I was hoping you'd turn up."

Dev was amazed at the way Anya's brown eyes lit up as she tilted her head at him and asked, "Were you?"

He grinned at her. "You mean you weren't expecting me?"

Anya shook her head, her brilliant white teeth biting into her luscious lower lip. "No."

"I'll go then," said Dev, turning around, without taking a single step forward, hoping that she would stop him.

He was not disappointed when Anya said, "Please don't," with a hand on his arm. Her touch sizzled across his skin, giving him goose bumps.

Dev caught Anya's trembling hand and turned back to her, the smile disappearing from his grey eyes when he saw the expression on her face. "Anya…" His touch as light as a feather, he traced the side of her face, fascinated with the curl of dark, silky hair which clung to his forefinger.

He looked down at her face which was softly lit by the moonlight. Her rosy lips were parted as she seemed to have difficulty with her breathing. And her chest heaved. Dev eyed her breasts for a couple of seconds before lifting his gaze back to her face.

Will she let him kiss her? Well, he had to try, now or never. She was definitely attracted to him, even if not as much as he was entranced by her.

Dev took her small chin between his thumb and forefinger, bringing her face closer to his. "Anya… you don't know how tempting you are. I…"

He was surprised when she suddenly went up on her toes before placing her hands firmly on his shoulders. And then it happened, the kiss he had been thinking about for the past few minutes. Anya took the initiative, pressing her soft lips to his. Unable to resist, Dev gathered her in his arms, pulling her close against his body before tracing the shape of her delicious lips with his tongue.

Dev felt himself drowning in sensations which he had never experienced before, as her innocent lips fluttered against his. On the verge of losing himself, he suddenly came to his senses and jerked away from her, removing her hands from his shoulders. "My God! Anya…" The words were torn from him as Dev shook his head, colour running up his cheeks.

Dev had had his quota of girlfriends, but had never, ever, felt this way in his life—as if his whole body was burning up with need. He had to leave before the situation blew completely out of control. "Good night, Anya." Dev walked away from her, jumping over the wall, and going towards the staircase with a small wave.

He did his best to keep away from the terrace over the next few days, too disturbed by his raging emotions. Raging hormones he could handle, but emotions were a different ballgame. He could not face those now, not when he was on the threshold of setting up his farm, against so many odds. Dev was extremely focussed that way. And Anya was a teenager, damn it! He could do without the complication right now.

On the following Wednesday night, Durgesh started the topic of marriage at the dinner table. "Dev, I spoke to Anya's father in Chandigarh. They are keen to get her married off. She is an only child, by the way, from a very well-to-do family. She is also educated, actually smart enough to bag a seat in MBA. They are also keen to have an alliance with our family. But..."

Dev glared at his father, a heavy frown on his face. He placed a hand against his chest, as if to tell his heart to shut up. "Dad, I don't want to get married at this point in my life. I'm barely twenty-five. Not for another five years at least. Right now, my focus is only my farm. There's too much to do. I won't have time for a wife or family."

"That's another thing I wanted to talk to you about. Anya's father was thrilled to know that you are also well qualified and is eager to take this forward. But one thing though..."

"Dad, did you even hear me?" asked Dev, his scowl turning fiercer.

"Of course, I did," said Durgesh. "It is you who's not listening to me. You can get engaged for now and get married a couple of years later, if you prefer." Karishma had been convinced that their son was attracted to the Madhvanis' guest and Durgesh was keen to strike the iron while it was hot—anything to get his son away from the madness of farming. When Dev did not respond, he continued, "Her parents are really excited to get their daughter tied up with a boy from Mumbai, especially one who is... who is..." He turned to look at his wife.

Karishma started from where her husband had left off. "It is like this Dev. They are keen to go ahead with the alliance if you have a job with an MNC."

"You guys aren't serious, are you?" asked Dev, his voice having gone quiet, even as his temper rose diametrically. So that was how it was going to be. Anya and her parents had sided with his mother and father to force him to give up his idea of becoming a farmer. Wasn't it a good thing that he had decided to stay away from her?

"Of course, we are, Dev. What do you think?" flared his father. "We have only your best interests at heart. Both your mother and I are keen that you settle down, that you have a good life…"

"…and you believe that I don't have a good life as of now. Dad, Mom, let's get this clear once and for all. I don't plan to change my mind. I'm going ahead with my career in farming. If it really irritates the hell out of you guys, I'll move out of our home," said Dev. Maybe it was best if he did just that. He could rent a house in Karjat, not far from his farm, until his farmhouse was ready. The foundation was already being laid and it would probably take another eight months at the most. And living close to the farm would definitely be an advantage.

Durgesh lost it. "Do that. Struggling by yourself will probably knock some sense into you."

Dev stared at his father, nodding slowly. "Okay, give me two days and I'll get out of your hair."

It was a week of upheaval and Dev kept shutting away the picture of Anya which kept popping into his mind. Anya was not for him—not today, not in the future. Not if she wanted him to change his mind about his career.

Even before he moved out of his parents' home, Dev got to know that Anya had left her uncle's place to return to her hometown. Good! That should shut his heart up completely. And to be truthful, he really did not have the time or the energy to be in a relationship, not when Wadhwa Farm was still in the nascent stage.

It was not long before Anya became a forgotten dream or so believed Dev, only to find out that she promptly popped to the surface of his mind every time he met an attractive woman. And Dev realised over time that he could not connect with any other woman emotionally, not with the lovely Anya buried somewhere deep within his heart.

7

It was Monday afternoon by the time the police connected Anya Chhabria's name to the accident victim. Even then, they were not sure. Police Inspector Borkar was under tremendous pressure what with the call from the Police Commissioner's office. He had an assistant dig out Wadhwa's contact number and called him.

"*Arre* Wadhwa, *mein* Inspector Borkar," he growled into his phone, his ego taking a dent. But then, he wanted to do it personally so that it earned him a brownie point in the Commissioner's eyes, or so he hoped.

"*Haan* sir, *boliye*," said Dev, hoping against hope that the man had got a lead.

"That woman who got hurt in the car accident that day, do you know where she is?"

"*Ji*, she's in the hospital, getting treatment." Dev was not keen to divulge too much to the man as he did not trust him at all.

"Do you know which hospital?"

"Why, sir? Is someone asking for her?"

"Look here, Wadhwa. I am asking the questions here. Which hospital is the victim in?"

"Leelavati Hospital." Dev was getting angry by the minute.

Inspector Borkar disconnected the phone without saying another word, much to Dev's chagrin. The bastard!

Dev called out, "Come in," when there was a knock at the door. In walked Nurse Saldana along with Inspector Borkar and two other men. Dev got up, his stance threatening. "I don't think the patient is ready to meet so many people." He stopped them in the middle of the room, not allowing them to walk any further. He did not want Anya to undergo more trauma than what she was already suffering from.

"He's right," said the man wearing a ponytail. "Hello, I'm Arth Sharma and this is Farhan Merchant, my partner. I hear that you've already met Inspector Borkar," he said, shaking Dev's hand. He turned to the policeman and said, "Why don't the two of us wait outside?"

While Borkar did not like it one bit, he was not left with a choice as he knew that it was Arth Sharma who knew the Police Commissioner personally. He walked out with Sharma and the nurse, giving Dev Wadhwa an angry glance.

Farhan spoke softly, a tremor in his voice. "It's Anya."

Dev's head jerked towards him. "You know her?"

"I was married to her until a few days ago. And we were besties from kindergarten." Farhan rubbed a hand over his eyes. "Did she open her eyes at all since the accident?" He walked slowly towards the bed, staring at the fragile woman sleeping there.

Anya had been married? Well, she must have been, of course. Her parents had been on the lookout for a suitable groom for her even five years back. But that still did not stop Dev from being shocked. And now she was divorced too. Why was that? Had her marriage not been a happy one? His heart beat hard as Dev stared at Farhan. "What do you mean you were married until a few days back? Aren't you her husband anymore?"

Farhan did not take his eyes off Anya. "We got divorced at the Bandra family court on Friday morning. If I understand it right, she met with the accident immediately after she left the court."

"And where the hell were you at that time?" Dev did not know why he was angry with Farhan. But he was. The other man had known Anya all her life and had even been married to her for a couple of years. Dev realised that he did not like it one bit.

Farhan turned to give Dev a sad look. "That's exactly what I'm cursing myself for. I left the court a few minutes later. I saw there had been an accident, but also noticed someone—I think it was you—had taken over. I rushed away as I never even imagined it could be Anya."

Dev could see that the other man was genuine. "Sit down," he said, pointing to the sofa and handing Farhan a glass of water. "I'm glad you came. I only knew Anya by her first name and was puzzled as to how I was going to contact her family. Searching for only the first name on social media," Dev rolled his eyes, "must be the most difficult task."

Gulping a mouthful of water thirstily, Farhan asked in a broken voice, "You mean Anya hasn't opened her eyes in all these four days?"

Dev sighed. "She did. But she can't recall who she is."

"What?" Farhan looked shaken. "What does that mean? She has no memory?"

Dev nodded. "Yes, she has absolutely no memory of her past, not even her own name."

"Oh my God!" Farhan held his head. "My poor Anya. What a mess!"

His poor Anya? Dev frowned heavily. *Didn't he just say that they were divorced?*

"If you'll excuse me a minute, I need to call her parents." Farhan took out his cell phone to call Gaurav Chhabria. "Uncle, *main* Farhan. Anya is unwell and that's why her phone was switched off. I think it would be for the best if you and Aunty came to Mumbai."

"What? What's wrong with Anya? You didn't mention anything before now." Gaurav was more irritated than anxious.

"That's because I didn't know she was so ill."

"Let me give the phone to Aunty," said Gaurav, calling out to his wife. Without bothering that he might be heard, he told Amal, "I don't understand these modern couples. Farhan says Anya is ill, and we should go to Mumbai immediately. But he didn't know that she was ill before now. What kind of man doesn't know when his wife has taken ill?"

Amal grabbed the phone from her husband to shout at Farhan, "What happened? What is wrong with Anya? Tell me Farhan." She began to wail loudly, beating against her chest.

"Aunty, please calm down." Farhan could not face the drama. Poor Anya! She could do without this. But how could he stop her parents from visiting her? She was seriously ill and he was not left with a choice but to inform them.

Amal ranted and raved for a while before Farhan told her that he needed to attend to the sick Anya. "It would be best if you and Uncle came to Mumbai immediately." He disconnected the phone, unable to take any more.

"So, do you still love her?" asked Dev, wondering why they were divorced.

Farhan turned to him with a jerk of his head, as if he had forgotten that Dev was in the same room. "You mean Anya? Yes, I've always loved her. I told you that she is my best friend." He turned when he saw a movement in his peripheral. Anya was awake.

A slender man walked close to her and held her left hand, the one free of needles, in both of his. He looked upset, his eyes red from tears or maybe lack of sleep, she could not say.

"Anya, I'm so glad to see you awake. You gave me such a fright. I had almost given you up for dead." He made an effort to keep his voice from breaking.

She looked at the man's kind face. What was he doing in her hospital room? Did he know her? He had called her Anya.

"We know each other?" she asked, a befuddled expression on her pale features.

It was with great difficulty that Farhan stopped himself from breaking down as he nodded. "Yes, I've known you since you were three years old."

Panic flooded Anya's face as she turned to look for the one familiar face she had come to depend upon since waking up in the hospital bed. "Dev!" she called out to him.

Dev could not help the joy which burst forth in his heart that it was he who Anya wanted by her side as he walked over to her swiftly, touching her shoulder reassuringly. "This is Farhan Merchant. He says you were married to him."

Anya looked at Farhan again with disturbed brown eyes. "Are you my husband?" Somehow, she could not think of him as her husband.

Farhan shook his head. "Not any more. We're divorced."

"Why? We didn't get along?" asked Anya, curious.

Farhan gave her a bitter smile. "We got along like a house on fire. That wasn't the issue." He looked at Dev, wondering if he should continue to talk in front of the stranger. But what the hell, Dev Wadhwa had saved Anya's life and had obviously taken care of her for four days. "I'm gay, Anya. Despite knowing that, my parents were insistent that I get married to a woman. And you, my BFF, were being pressured by your parents to get married. The two of us decided to tie the knot to shut them all up. We were married in name only, for two years. A few months ago, I met Arth and fell in love. That was when we decided to get a divorce. On Friday, the divorce was finalised. You had the accident immediately after you left the court, on your way back home."

Anya was listening avidly, but as one would listen to a story of someone else's life. She felt absolutely no connection to his tale.

Dev felt humongous relief when he heard what Farhan had to say. Anya was a free woman now; one he could pursue if he wanted to as Farhan had never had a romantic interest in her.

Dev needed to know Anya more. But her parents would be arriving soon. Will he get a chance? Or will they whisk her away to God knew where? No, he would not let her disappear from his life this time round. This time, Dev decided to listen to his heart and allow his raging emotions to reign supreme.

8

All hell broke loose during the visiting hours on Tuesday morning. Amal and Gaurav had arrived at the hospital and entered Anya's room, resembling two bulls in a China shop. All the nurse's requests for silence fell on deaf ears as Amal howled her heart out. She had only then got to know that her daughter had been in an accident.

She turned to give Farhan a furious glare. "Why didn't you tell us before Farhan? You think we didn't have a right to know?"

He did not reply, as he had nothing to say that would calm her down. He just stared back at her stonily.

Amal dropped her gaze to walk towards her daughter who was lying on the hospital bed. And who was that standing beside her? It was a stranger holding her hand.

Gaurav beat his wife to it when he asked, "Who are you, young man?" looking pointedly at his hand lying in Anya's hold.

"Hello sir, I'm Dev Wadhwa."

Anya gave Dev a panicked look, unable to recognise the older couple. Who were they? And what were they doing in her hospital room? Her grip tightened on his hand.

"Anya," cried Amal, "what happened to you?" She stared at Anya who appeared pathetically pale and thin. How bad had the accident been? Farhan had not mentioned any bones being broken, only a knock to her head. Had she recovered now?

"Who are you?" asked Anya, returning the other woman's stare with equal fervour. She felt intimidated, what with being unable to recognise the couple and the strong—even threatening—vibes emanating from them.

"What?" shrieked Amal, her eyes almost popping out of her head. She turned to look at her husband, who appeared stunned, before returning her gaze to Anya. "I'm your mother. I held you in my womb for all of nine months and gave birth to you after suffering such long labour pains and you ask me who I am?" She wanted to shake Anya.

Dev raised a hand to stop the flow of words, his temper building. What was wrong with the woman? Couldn't she see that her daughter had undergone a traumatic accident? He met Farhan's eyes over Anya's parents' heads and saw the other man shake his own, a bitter expression on his face. "Ma'am, I suppose you don't realise how ill your daughter is. I…"

"And how would you know, Mr. Wadhwa?" asked Gaurav, desperate to find a punching bag.

Farhan could not stop himself from intervening. "Uncle, Aunty, listen. Dev was the one who found Anya after her accident. He's the one who's been tending to her for five days. She…"

"And where were you all that time?" Gaurav turned his angry brown gaze on his son-in-law. Yes, he was still not aware that Anya and Farhan were divorced.

"I want to be left alone," said Anya, her voice stronger than ever before. Before anyone could answer her, she rang the bell for the nurse. When Nurse Saldana walked in, Anya said, "Can you please ask all these people to leave my room? I'm tired and need to sleep." She did not bother to even look in the older couple's direction. The woman called herself her mother. And the man was probably her father. But Anya could not connect with either of them, not one little bit. She was terribly scared that she could not recognise her own parents. It was all the worse because she felt no feeling other than fear.

Amal began to wail when Nurse Saldana attempted to escort them all out. "You ungrateful child! How dare you turn away from your own parents? You…"

"Ma'am," said the nurse gently. "Anya ma'am is suffering from amnesia. She can't recognise anyone. She…"

"What the hell do you mean she can't recognise anyone? We are her parents, damn it!" Gaurav burst out angrily, glaring at the woman.

Nurse Saldana's stance became aggressive. "Sir, madam, I think it is best you talk to Dr. Adnani. The patient's health is most important to us. If there is going to be any disruption to that, I might have to call security." She pinned Amal and Gaurav with her stern gaze, showing them she meant business.

Gaurav escorted a muttering Amal out of the hospital room, almost bursting a blood vessel. "Show us to the doctor. I'll give him a piece of my mind."

"You might have to check at the reception for an appointment, sir," said Nurse Saldana sternly.

"You come with us, Farhan," ordered Gaurav, on his way to the elevator bank.

The two of them kept firing questions at Farhan on their way down. He continued to look at them stonily, refusing to rise to their baits. He had done his best to explain to them that Anya was suffering from memory loss. They obviously could not understand what that meant. They had gathered that she had not broken any bones and hence concluded that there was nothing wrong with her. He had given up after a while, allowing them to find out for themselves.

They reached the reception and Gaurav demanded an audience with Dr. Adnani. He was politely told that he could meet the specialist after a couple of hours. No amount of arguing made the receptionist budge. "I'm sorry sir, but the doctor has appointments lined up continuously. I can ensure a ten-minute slot just before he goes on his rounds." Even that could be made possible only because the doctor had left instructions that he wanted to meet Anya Chhabria's family, if and when they turned up.

Gaurav gave her a curt nod before turning to Amal and Farhan. "It's still visiting hours, right? Let's go meet Anya."

"Uncle, please understand that Anya is ill. We need to remain calm while visiting her," pleaded Farhan.

Gaurav frowned at his son-in-law. "Tell me what you are doing with us down here, when that Dev Wadhwa is holding your wife's hand and staying by her side?"

Stumped for a second, Farhan thought on his feet. "But Uncle, you only told me to come down here with you."

"But what is that man doing by my daughter's bedside?"

"Shall we go to the canteen? We are in everyone's way," requested Farhan. Anya's father insisted on speaking loudly however much Farhan lowered his voice. And people had begun to stare at them.

Amal wiped her face with a handkerchief, sniffing loudly. "I could do with a cup of tea. Let's go."

With a sigh of relief, Farhan escorted them to the back of the building and seated them at a table, before going to the self-service counter to buy three cups of tea.

Sipping from his cup, Gaurav continued with his interrogation. "Where were you when Anya had the accident?"

"I was at work." Farhan lied through his teeth, not daring to tell the other man the truth. He was not going back on his promise to Anya, to keep the divorce a secret from her parents.

"But later? You told us only last night that she was ill."

"Anya was going out for the weekend with her friends. But the accident happened and they could not find any identification on her. Even when she woke up, she could not remember anything and so the hospital could not inform her family." Farhan felt terrible about it, despite Arth and Dev having reassured him that there was not much he could have done under the circumstances. It was a quirk of destiny that things had happened the way they had. But that did not stop Farhan from feeling guilty.

"But I don't understand," said Amal, "Anya looks totally normal. You saw how she shouted at us to get out of her room. That's her normal behaviour, no respect for her parents or elders at all. I can't believe that she is unable to recognise us. That's such a strange diagnosis."

"Aunty, I think it is best if Dr. Adnani explains it all to you. I also only understand to some extent as I'm not an expert."

"I still don't know what Dev Wadhwa is doing with her. Did Anya know him from before?"

Farhan shook his head. "No Uncle. Dev happened to be at the scene of the accident. He had only gone with her to the hospital in the ambulance. When the police could not find who the accident victim was, Dev stayed back to care for her and even paid the hospital bill. He was the first person she saw when she opened her eyes. It's understandable that she has become attached to him."

Gaurav's scowl turned blacker as he did not like what his son-in-law was saying. How can his married daughter get close to a strange man? And Farhan did not seem to mind. He just could not relate to this modern generation at all. He said, "*Arre,* they must have definitely found her cell phone or her handbag. There must have been some kind of identification. The police are also dumb."

Did the man even listen when anyone spoke? Farhan had told him at least four times that Anya's car had been flattened and her phone had been in smithereens. He had also explained that they could not find her handbag or any papers. Just now, he simply nodded, saving his breath.

The three of them waited to meet the doctor, Farhan having the most difficult time as Anya's parents continued to shoot questions at him, most of them repetitive.

9

nya held back the tears which were pushing against her closed eyelids. But one escaped and ran down the left side, falling into her pillow. What was wrong with her? How much ever she strained her brain, her mind, she could not recall anything, not even her parents. Everything was blank. She only knew her life from the moment she had opened her eyes on her hospital bed. She supposed she must thank God for Dev's presence. Though he had mentioned that they had met before, they obviously had not known each other well. Otherwise, he would have known her surname and would have had her cell number.

What did all that matter anyway? Anya could not remember anyone from her life prior to her accident. Considering that, she knew Dev better than the few others who had walked into her present life. Farhan seemed nice. He had spent a couple of hours with her, when Dev had had to run on an urgent errand yesterday.

"We grew up together, Anya," Farhan had said in a gentle voice. "We met on the first day in Junior KG, at a small school in Chandigarh. You were chubby and cute, wearing two plaits. The boys were aggressive and I preferred to spend time with you."

Anya nodded, listening, trying to recall the scene. Blank!

"We studied together till the tenth standard. After that, you went on to do Commerce in Junior College and then BMS, while I did Arts and BMM, though we continued to study in the same college."

Anya listened avidly. He seemed to have been with her throughout her life. Did they love each other? Somehow, he felt more like a sibling than a lover. She nodded again, waiting for him to continue.

"You know something," Farhan's voice turned softer than ever, "You were the first one to know that I was gay." His eyes turned gentle as he looked at her. "You never judged me. While my parents wanted to kill me and several of my friends disappeared from my life, you, Anya, were the only one who stood by me." He got emotional. "You were the one who gave me the strength to accept myself for what I am."

Anya's eyes went wide. Farhan was gay and she had known about it. But her mind still drew a blank at the thought.

"There was tremendous pressure from my parents, for me to get married. They did not give me a choice as I'm their eldest born. And there you were, undergoing a similar experience, all because you were an only child. Your parents were also insistent that you get married. We had just turned twenty-two, and it was like facing bull-dozers. Our respective parents were wearing out our strong stance. I didn't want to cheat a woman into marrying me, when my inclinations were otherwise. You didn't want to get married just for the heck of it, to some stranger. That was when we both cooked up an idea between us."

His eyes turned mischievous, surprising her. Farhan had seemed like a serious type of person until then. "What did we do?" she asked him.

"We got married to each other," he laughed. "Seriously, that's what we did," he said, seeing her startled look. "Although in name only. We were two friends setting out to rescue one another from a dire situation. And it worked. My parents weren't happy that I was marrying a non-Parsi and they cut off their relationship with me. I tried to keep in touch but gave up after many failed attempts. Anyway, they never cared for my way of life; nor did they accept that I am gay. Your parents didn't mind your tying the knot with me, even if I didn't belong to your Sindhi community. All they wanted was for someone to marry you and take you off their hands as you were already twenty-two."

Anya stared at him, listening to the bizarre story. "We got married when I was twenty-two? But that's so young. Why did my parents want to get rid of me? Was I such a troublesome daughter?" she asked, her voice small. Though she could not remember a damn thing, Anya somehow found it difficult to relate to herself as a troublemaker. She had not had any urge to be aggressive over the past two days.

Farhan shook his head vigorously. "Your parents didn't want to get rid of you. They wanted to marry you off since every girl in your extended family was married off by the time she turned twenty. You were the one who got to be a spinster till the ripe age of twenty-two," he grinned. "And as for being a troublesome daughter, you were anything but that. You were chirpy, happy-go-lucky, and just wanted to live your life. You had a rocking career. After BMS, you went on to do an MBA. We got married immediately after that and now you know why. We both shifted to Mumbai, more for getting away from our families than for any other reason. You took up a job with a private company and had been doing extremely well there."

"Oh my God! Do the people in my office know that I've had an accident? I..." She bit her lip, a bitter expression on her face. "I can't recall a damn thing," she growled.

"I called up your boss and told him about your accident and that... you can't remember anything as of now. I..."

Anya placed her hands at the sides of her head, holding it gingerly, careful of not touching the stitches at the back. "Right now, it feels like I'm never going to remember anything. Whenever I try to reach within my mind, I feel as if... as if I'm walking through a cloud. Do you understand what I mean? There seems to be a substance that appears out of reach, until I wade through it. And then what? Just nothing."

Farhan held her hand in both of his. "Anya, sweetie, please don't fret. Allow your body to heal first. And then..."

"And then what?" She glared at him. "Do you know Dr. Adnani says that he cannot guarantee that I'll ever regain my memory?"

Farhan looked into her stormy brown eyes for a few seconds before nodding slowly. "Yes, I know. But then, we must live in hope, right? How else can we survive?"

She lifted a hand to wipe away an angry tear which rolled down her right cheek. No, she will not cry. As if that helped anyone, ever. "Go on with your—our—story. So, are we still husband and wife?"

"We got divorced barely half an hour before your accident. You see, I met Arth, my lover and partner, a few months ago. And the time had come for you and me to part ways. You don't know how glad I was—I am—that I hadn't seriously got tied with a girl in marriage."

"So, you have moved in with Arth?"

"Yes, and the apartment we both used to live in, is all yours."

Anya's eyes darkened. While it was good to know that she had a place to go to, it was not easy being completely unaware of how the place looked.

Seeing her expression, Farhan's hold on her hand tightened. "Do you want me to shift back home with you? I can, as long as you need me."

She shook her head. "No Farhan. It must be barely a few days since you moved in with your new partner. I don't want you to rock that boat for my sake." Anya was clear about that.

"What will you do? Go live with your parents then?" he asked, worried about her.

Anya gave him a bitter smile. "Who are my parents? I don't know anyone." It was only Dev she knew. It was only Dev she felt safe with.

Anya came back to the present, wiping one more tear which had followed the first. Meeting her parents had only reinstated her decision. The woman who had called herself her mother had not even given her a hug.

And the man with her—supposedly her father—had only a frown to offer. She simply felt no connection with them. Shouldn't she have felt some kind of a spark? Something to show that they were connected by blood? It was so frustrating that Anya felt nothing for them.

Amal Chhabria sat crying beside her husband as Dr. Adnani spoke to Anya's parents. Farhan sat in the third chair, silently listening. "Mr. Chhabria, the brain is a sensitive organ. When your daughter Anya had the accident, she hit her head against the divider; that is what Mr. Dev Wadhwa told us. She was lucky to have had him around to help her. You may have heard of several cases where victims lie on the road without help for hours together. We have conducted all possible tests and have given her the best treatment that our hospital has to offer. She was in a coma until two days ago. It was only after she woke up when we realised that she had no memory of her past."

Gaurav looked at the doctor with a heavy frown, trying to grasp the meaning of his words. "How is that possible, doctor? She hurt her head and her brain. How can that impact her mind? Isn't it the mind that holds the thoughts?"

"We can argue about this forever, Mr. Chhabria, and still not arrive at a definite answer. According to science, your daughter has had a head injury which has affected her memory. To put it in layman's terms, let us look at it like this... the brain and mind work in tandem, one helping the other. So, a disturbance in one, impacts the other. Since her brain is hurt, it has disturbed her mind…"

"Then shouldn't we assume that once her brain is healed, her memory should return?" asked Gaurav shrewdly.

Amal looked from one man to another, feeling the tension roiling within her.

"Ideally yes," said Dr. Adnani. "But going by past history, I cannot promise such a result. The wound heals, of course. But obviously, the impact continues till the time the patient regains her memory. Well, to be truthful, there have been a few case histories where the patients never remembered their pasts."

"Are you saying that my daughter might never recall who she is?" Amal asked, her voice dangerously soft.

"Yes, Mrs. Chhabria, that's what I am saying," said the doctor, a look of relief on his face. It had not been easy dealing with Anya's parents. It never was easy, handling the family of amnesia patients and he had seen a few in his lifetime. But these two were the most difficult.

Amal got up, pushing her chair back noisily. "We understand that this hospital is not good enough for us. We would like to move Anya out immediately and shift her to a better one."

Farhan and the doctor looked on in shock when Amal walked out of the cabin with Gaurav in tow.

"But it's too early to discharge her," said the doctor to Farhan, a worried frown on his face. "I don't want Anya to become more ill than she already is."

Farhan straightened his shoulders, as if getting ready for battle. "No worries there, Doctor. Anya's parents believe that she is still married to me. I'll take the decisions, as her husband."

Dr. Adnani's eyes twinkled behind his spectacles as he gave a small nod to the young man.

"Uncle, Aunty," called out Farhan, catching up with the older couple as they continued to walk to the reception. He guided them to a corner and made them sit down. "Anya is too ill to be discharged. I…"

"But the doctor is an idiot for all we know. Amal is right. It is best to get a second opinion," said Gaurav. He did not like the situation one bit. "Anya has medical insurance, right?" he asked.

Farhan found the opportunity he was looking for. "But Uncle, we've spent more than the insurance cover. And…"

"See, I told you. They are cheats, all of them," declared Amal in an angry voice.

Farhan could see Anya's father's mind working. Her parents were not all that rich. "But Uncle, *achcha khasa* treatment is going on here. Why do you want to change things at this point? Dr. Adnani has literally pulled Anya out of the jaws of death," he exaggerated. "If we take her to another hospital now, they will again want to do all the scans and tests. We'll be spending double the money. For all you know, the doctors there will also say the same thing." He drove his point home, looking only at Gaurav and not Anya's mother.

Gaurav could see Farhan's point. "So, what do you suggest?"

Farhan gave a sigh of relief. "Let Anya become physically healed. I'll take her home after that, give it some time and maybe go for some other treatment if things don't change." He knew that after today's fiasco there was not a chance in hell that Anya would go to live with her parents.

Amal began to cry. "What are we going to do? That girl doesn't want us. She never did like us," she wailed.

Farhan came to a quick decision. "Aunty, will you please take my advice?" When she nodded, he continued, "You and Uncle are too old for this trauma. I called you here only because you might want to see Anya after the major accident she had. But now she is on the road to recovery and there isn't much you can do here. I think it is best you go back home."

"What?" asked Gaurav, "Are you sure you can manage? And what about that Dev Wadhwa? What if he interferes?"

"It's not a question of Dev interfering, Uncle. He has been a help throughout. I'll manage, you don't worry."

Gaurav turned to look at Amal. "What do you say?"

She sniffed. "It's obvious that we aren't wanted here. So, it is best we go. But Farhan, do bring Anya home if she wants to come. Our doors are always open for the two of you," she declared dramatically.

"Of course, Aunty," said Farhan, hugging her. "Would you like me to book your tickets?" he asked solicitously, keen to have them out of his hair at the earliest.

"Could you do that? Thanks," said Gaurav.

Farhan ensured that they left within the hour, to stay in the airport VIP lounge, so that they could catch the early morning flight the next day.

Breathing a sigh of relief after he seated the two of them in a cab, he went to Anya's room to see how she was faring.

Opening the door, Farhan found Anya in Dev's arms. He left, closing the door silently behind him. It was obvious that the man had fallen for Anya in a big way. Farhan crossed his fingers, hoping that her life changed for the better from now on. Sending a WhatsApp message to Dev about Anya's parents being on their way home to Chandigarh, he left the premises, a smile on his lips.

11

Anya turned to the door when she heard it open. She smiled through her tears when she saw it was Dev. And what was he carrying? A bunch of flowers! When he got closer, she noticed that the bouquet of peach-coloured roses was beautifully put together along with white coloured baby's breath. The whole thing was tucked into a ceramic vase with a blue glaze. Anya's eyes shone with joy as she eyed the flowers.

"Are they for me, Dev? They look so lovely," she smiled broadly. "I love roses. They are my favourite flowers. Wherever did you find such fresh ones?"

Dev placed the vase on the table next to her bed, moving the table so that she could look at them whenever she was awake. He smiled back at her. "Roses are your favourite. Did you just remember that?" he asked.

Her eyes went wide in surprise as she turned from admiring the flowers to look at him. "Oh my God! You're right. I remembered something, didn't I? Oh Dev! You don't know how thrilled I am. Do you think I'll recall everything soon?"

He walked closer, taking her slender hand in his. "Let's believe that."

She held on to his hand, her grip a trifle desperate. "You never did tell me. Where did you find such fresh flowers?"

"I had them delivered from my farm in Karjat. They were plucked barely three hours ago."

"What are you saying?" Anya was excited. "Do you have a flower farm?"

"Yep, I do," he smiled at her indulgently. This was the first time she appeared excited about something. Her parents' visit had been pure drama. Thank God Farhan had accompanied them when the nurse shooed them both out.

"How lovely! What all do you grow there?" she asked.

Dev looked at her pale face, wanting to hold her close to his heart. Refraining himself, he said, "I grow roses in eleven different colours, there are gerberas, orchids, carnations, lilies, baby's breath, and a couple of other varieties... I think you should see them for yourself."

Her eyes had gone wide. "That's a lot of flowers. How big is your farm?"

He smiled. "Twenty-five acres. It's set close to the hills actually."

"Wow! I'd love to go there."

"That's exactly where I'm taking you once you're discharged from here." Living in nature was sure to heal her faster.

Her eyes turned wary. "Are you sure? Those two people who came today with Farhan... they said they were my parents. What if they make me go with them?" Her voice turned to a whisper. "I'm scared, Dev."

He pulled her into his arms, rubbing his chin on the top of her head, his large hands keeping her close to his heart in a secure hold. "No one will make you do anything you don't want to do." He lifted her chin to look down at her with a smile. "We know that you're not a minor, but all of twenty-four. You take your own decisions. If you want to go with me to my farm, then that is where you get to go."

"Who are all there in your home?" asked Anya.

"My grandmother's there. Then there are four dogs and a few cats. Six families live and work on the farm along with me. They have their own quarters on one corner of the property. What?" he asked, when her mouth opened wide.

She shook her head. "Nothing. I'm just surprised at how big your operation is. So many dogs, and cats too. I like cats," she declared.

"Cats and roses, just my kind of woman," he said, pressing his lips to her soft cheek, unable to stop himself.

Neither of them heard Farhan open the door and leave almost immediately, shutting it quietly behind him.

They sprang apart when Dev's phone pinged. He laid her back down gently on the bed before checking his phone. Farhan had sent him a message saying that Anya's parents were on their way back home to Chandigarh. Dev let out a sigh of relief. He looked at Anya but did not say anything when he saw her eyelids drooping.

12

It was Friday noon when Anya was discharged. Farhan had gone over to the hospital to help Dev get all the papers in order. He had also brought the original documents which he had for Anya's medical insurance, from her apartment. Farhan was happy to know that Anya was in safe hands when Dev told him that she was going to his farm in Karjat to recuperate.

"Let Anya remain there for a couple of months. Nothing like the fresh air and pampering to cure her of what's ailing her. Let's take a call after that," said Dev.

"Thanks buddy. You sure have taken a huge weight off my shoulders. Anya refused to let me stay with her at her apartment when I asked. I had been wondering what to do. I know for a fact that it was never a good idea to send her to her parents."

Dev grinned. "I agree with you on that point. Was she unhappy as a child?" he asked.

Farhan shrugged. "Not unhappy exactly. Just that there were too many restrictions which Anya did not care for." He smiled at Dev with a mischievous gleam in his eyes. "She got into a number of scrapes. I followed her everywhere and the two of us landed in trouble more times than I can count."

"You obviously rescued her from that life," said Dev.

"We rescued each other."

Farhan had brought Anya's clothes packed in a couple of suitcases and her laptop in its backpack. He had also purchased a smart phone for Anya and added his number, her parents' numbers, and those of their common friends. He handed the phone to Dev, saying, "I'm sure she'll find it useful."

"Of course," said Dev, tucking the phone in a side pouch on the backpack.

"Will Anya be able to take the long drive to Karjat?" asked Farhan.

"We are flying by helicopter from Juhu. No worries there."

"That's awesome, bro. Then allow me to give you both a ride to the heliport."

"That would be nice."

Farhan hugged Anya when she got out of his car at the heliport. "You take care, sweetie. And get well soon," he said.

Dev shook Farhan's hand. "You must visit us at the farm. And bring Arth along. You tell me when and I'll ask Shaan to pick you up," he offered.

"That would be great. I'll definitely take you up on your invitation the moment we can get away for a couple of days," said Farhan, touched by the offer.

He waved them away as Anya was safely tucked into the passenger's seat, moving away to get into his car when the rotor blades started circulating for takeoff.

Anya was excited about the helicopter ride. "I don't think I have been on one before," she chattered, "This is too much fun."

Dev gave her an indulgent glance, pointing out the mountain range they were crossing. They even saw a train chugging its way on a railway track.

She was surprised when they landed barely twenty-five minutes later, on a flat area marked with a huge W within a circle. Dev explained that the concrete helipad belonged to the Wadhwa Farm.

Anya's eyes went wide in surprise. "You have your own helipad? You mean you own this helicopter?"

Dev smiled, his teeth shining in the sunlight, as he nodded.

"Oh my God!" She pressed both her hands one on top of the other over her mouth. "You must be super rich."

"I suppose," said Dev, turning to look at the car which had come to pick them, colour running up his rugged cheeks. Lifting a hand to his farm manager who had accompanied the driver, he made the introductions. "Anya, this is Shaan, my manager. And Shaan, this is Anya."

"Hello!" Anya eyed Dev's manager warily. Finally concluding that he was non-threatening, she gave him a small smile.

"Hello, Anya. Welcome to Wadhwa Farm," said Shaan. "Let me get the luggage," said he, excusing himself.

Anya took in their surroundings. She could see a bungalow further down from where she stood, set against green hills in the background. There were a number of closed in structures, built at intervals. "What are those?" she asked, a frown of concentration on her face. "Hey, are they greenhouses?" she asked in excitement, when she thought she recognised them.

Dev turned towards her with a jerk. "You know what they are?"

She gave him a shy smile. "It seems so. Are they? Greenhouses, I mean."

"Yes, you can call them that. Actually, they are poly houses. I grow flowers in them."

Anya felt her heartbeat pick up in excitement. "How many flowers do you grow here?"

"Lots," he said, opening the door to the Innova Crysta which was parked nearby. Shaan had already loaded their luggage into the steel grey station wagon. Dev lifted Anya into the vehicle.

"Hey," she said, grabbing his neck. "You didn't have to do that."

He settled her in the seat, buckling the belt around her, giving her a sunny smile. "I know, but I wanted to. How are you feeling?" he asked, handing her a bottle of chilled juice.

"I think I'm fine. I don't think I must have travelled in such luxury, ever," she smiled, looking into his dark grey eyes.

"How would you know?" asked Dev, his smile turning wider, his teeth gleaming in the noon sunlight.

"Call it a woman's instinct," she said with an answering smile. His cheerful mood seemed to have rubbed off on her.

Dev laughed, shutting her door before walking to the other side and getting in beside her. "That's

Ramu *kaka*," he introduced the old man who was in the driver's seat. "Ramu *kaka*, this is Anya, my friend."

"*Namaste* Ramu *kaka*," said Anya, catching the smiling old eyes in the rear-view mirror as the driver nodded to her.

"Ramu *kaka* has been with our family since before I was born," said Dev.

Anya listened as the three men chatted, her head comfortably settled on Dev's shoulder as she closed her eyes.

It was barely ten minutes before the car stopped at the portico of the two-storey bungalow she had seen from the helipad. Anya opened her eyes to see a lovely structure, with wraparound verandas on both the ground and first floors. "Is this your home, Dev? It looks so serene and beautiful."

"It's your home too, Anya," said Dev, getting out to open her door.

She protested when he would have lifted her again. "No Dev, let me walk. I'm stronger than before."

"You sure?" he asked, a frown of concern on his face. She still looked pale.

"I promise to tell you if I can't, okay?"

He nodded, placing an arm around her shoulder, to escort her into his home. "*Daadima* must be waiting for us."

Anya gave him a worried look. "I hope she won't mind your bringing a stranger home to stay."

"Of course not..." They heard barking before he could finish what he was saying as four dogs came bounding towards them, their tails wagging vigorously.

Anya laughed, going on her knees on the ground, as they vied for her attention, licking her wherever they could reach. She placed her arms around two of them as the other two stepped on her thighs, wanting a cuddle too. "You cuties, you are so adorable," she crooned, rubbing her cheek against a silky black head.

Dev felt a flash of envy when he saw her gesture. "That's Tiger," he said, pointing to a brown and white dog, "and that's Blackie," who was completely black with soulful brown eyes. "The black and white dog is Gillie and the fully brown female is called Brownie. They are all mixed breed, strays who found their way into the farm."

"Oh, they look so healthy and are so friendly too." Anya continued to sit on the ground, unable to get up as the dogs wanted her attention in turns.

"Enough now," said Dev, whistling. The dogs immediately got off Anya to stand a couple of feet away, while their tails continued to wag. They looked at their master, as if awaiting further instructions. "I'm sure your lunch must also be served. Now go, all of you, time for food."

They took an about turn and ran enthusiastically towards a kennel that was further away, obviously having understood what Dev had said.

Anya laughed, getting to her feet. "They are all so cute," she said, dusting her jeans.

Dev smiled. "Wait till you meet the cats. But let's go meet *Daadima* and have lunch with her first." They removed their shoes at the entrance, before stepping inside. He guided her to a washroom, turning to the right wing once they stepped across the threshold.

Anya looked at her reflection in the mirror above the washbasin. Her face looked flushed and happy. Yes, she felt cheerful, especially after meeting the dogs. And Dev's place was so lush and green, with so many trees. She would need to check them at leisure. She was sure she had noticed some mangoes hanging from the branches. Maybe, just maybe, she might find peace here.

Anya studied her reflection in the mirror critically, all the more as she was going to meet Dev's grandmother. What would his grandmother think of his guest? Her injury was not obvious from the front. The hair at the back of her head had been shaven as the doctor had needed to stitch up the cut on her scalp where she had hit her head. While hair had begun to grow, it still looked ugly. Anya knew as she had insisted on Nurse Saldana holding the hand mirror behind her head when she had checked herself out in the hospital bathroom mirror.

Anya quickly splashed water on her face and wiped it with a towel. Brushing her hair back, she straightened her shoulders. It was time to go meet Dev's grandmother.

S tepping out of the bathroom, Anya looked at the inside of the house for the first time. Her mouth falling wide open, she stared at the open courtyard in the middle, with a wide corridor running around on the inside, parallel to the veranda opening into the compound. Carved wooden pillars surrounding the courtyard rose from the floor all the way to the wooden beams two storeys above, on which the tiled roof was structured.

Bright sunlight shone on the rough, red sandstone floor of the courtyard where flowering plants grew in abundance from where they were placed in large ceramic urns.

"Come with me," said Dev, appearing at her side and placing a hand at her elbow. They walked along the right fork of the square corridor surrounding the courtyard, moving towards the back where the matriarch of the family was sitting on a large, wooden swing which hung from the beamed rafters, her back straight, her keen eyes trained on their guest.

"*Daadima*, this is Anya Chhabria, and Anya, this is my grandmother, Meena Wadhwa, my most favourite person on earth," introduced Dev.

"*Namaste* Aunty," said Anya, looking at the old lady's wrinkled face with a wary expression in her brown eyes.

"*Sindhi aahein?*" *Daadima* asked Anya, a gentle smile on her face.

"*Ji,*" said Anya, a little of her nervousness fading away.

Meena let out a merry laugh, patting the empty seat next to her on the swing. "*Sindhi paryaan padra!*" She continued to laugh and Anya felt herself warming up to her.

"That's so true, *Auntyji*," nodded Anya, sitting next to the old lady and giving her a soft smile, "One can definitely identify a Sindhi from afar."

"*Daadima* loves to talk in Sindhi. But almost all the workers on the farm are locals, and she kind of misses conversing in her mother tongue." Dev told Anya as he sat down on a comfortable chair placed nearby, out of the swing's path.

"Dev tells me that you haven't been keeping well," said Meena, running a gentle hand over Anya's taut and tense back. "Staying at the farm amidst the lush greenery will get you well soon, *beta*. And you must call me *Daadima* too," she said in a gentle but firm voice.

Anya nodded mutely.

"Dev, will you ask Seema to serve lunch? I'm sure you both must be hungry."

"It's done, *Daadima*. Seema Aunty must be bringing the food out as we talk."

Just then, Anya noticed a woman come out of a room, presumably the kitchen, which was on their right, and place two serving bowls on the dining table which was set on the other side of the courtyard.

"Come *beta*," said *Daadima*, getting down from the swing. She looked diminutive compared to her tall grandson who was six feet, two inches in his socks. Even Anya appeared tall beside her, measuring five feet, seven inches.

Dev walked between the two women, his arms around their shoulders as they went to the dining table. He pulled the chair at the head for *Daadima* to sit, before pulling out the one on her right for Anya, her chair facing the courtyard. After she was seated comfortably, Dev went to sit on his grandmother's left side, opposite Anya.

Anya stared at the riot of colours which splashed across the open courtyard. There were roses, hibiscus, oleanders, gerbera, and carnations, in many shades. They were so pleasing to the eye. It must be such a joy living in this house.

They did not talk much as they tucked into the lunch of *roti, chicken curry, mixed veg gravy* and *jeera rice*. The food was spicy and yummy, accompanied by thick curds, slices of onion and roasted *papad*. Though she took only small helpings, Anya relished every bite she ate.

Sitting back to sip from her glass of water, Anya said, "Thank you so much *Daadima*, for having me here." She managed to stop her voice from breaking with emotion, as she felt like a piece of driftwood in the middle of a stormy sea, with no memories to hold on to.

"*Arre*, not at all *beta*, you are welcome to make your home with us." Meena had taken an instant liking to the waiflike woman who had walked into their home. And she could see that her grandson was completely enamoured by Anya. The old lady thought that maybe she could dare to dream of seeing her grandson finally getting married. He was almost thirty and refused to let anyone speak of his taking a bride. Meena could not help but notice how Dev's eyes followed Anya's every movement.

"Ah!" Anya moved her chair away in a hurry when she felt something furry brush against her bare foot. She bent down to look under the dining table to see a fluffy ginger cat sitting comfortably on her left foot. "Oh my God! And who's this?" she asked, gurgling with laughter. She bent down to stroke a light finger over the top of the feline's velvety head.

Dev bent down to check before saying, "That's Ginger, the lord of the manor."

"You mean there's a lady too?" asked Anya, giving the cat a good rub as he climbed up her leg to settle on her lap.

"Oh yes, and she has delivered a litter of three kittens the day before yesterday," said Meena.

"Kittens?" Anya gave Meena a dazzling smile, the first since she had entered their home. "Will the new mother let me near them?" she asked in awe.

"Why not?" smiled Meena indulgently, happy to notice that their guest obviously loved animals. "Dev, Kitty is settled on the top floor of the dog's kennel along with her little ones. Why don't you take Anya over to see the lot? And Anya, would you like to name the kittens?" asked Grandma.

"Oh, may I?" squealed Anya in delight.

"Later," said Dev firmly. "You need to have your medicines and take some rest first, Anya."

"Please Dev," said Anya. "After we see the kittens?"

Dev shook his head. "Dr. Adnani made me promise that I'd take good care of you. Only on that condition did he allow your discharge from the hospital. I'm sure the cats must all be fast asleep now, in the middle of the day," he insisted. "They will wake up to play after five. You rest for some time and then I promise to take you to see them first thing after you wake up," he said firmly.

Anya pouted at him, not protesting as she felt tired suddenly. "You're right. I feel beat," she said.

"Here, give Ginger to me," said Meena, lifting the sleeping cat from Anya's lap lovingly. "I'm also going to take a nap. Will catch up with you later in the evening, Anya. You take rest."

Anya got up from her chair and clutched the table when she swayed on her feet. Dev was beside her the very next second, lifting her up in his arms. "*Chalo*, nap time," he said, nodding to his grandmother, before walking towards the staircase near the entrance.

Anya did not protest as she locked weak arms around his neck, her head falling back against his chest. "I'm sorry," she mumbled.

"For what?" asked Dev, an indulgent smile on his face as his heart swelled with emotion.

"That you have to carry me around. I promise to get well soon, Dev."

"I like holding you in my arms, Anya," said Dev in a whisper, his lips brushing against her ear as he reached the first floor. He walked down the left corridor which had a wooden railing on the right, looking down on the plant-filled courtyard. Not that Anya really noticed much as he went to the third doorway which lay open. He walked in to place Anya down on the four-poster bed. He took her medicines out of the small pouch which was placed on a side table. Removing three pills on his palm, he took a glass of water and made the half-asleep Anya swallow them. He patted her back to ensure that they had all gone down before letting her lie down on her pillow.

"Do you want me to help you out of your jeans?" he asked solicitously.

"Hmm…" She stared at him uncomprehendingly, her eyes open barely a slit.

Dev smiled, bending down to kiss her on her petal soft cheek. "Go to sleep," he ordered, removing her belt before pulling a thin comforter over her.

She was fast asleep even before he stepped out of the door. He left the double door open, just in case she called out, before going down the staircase.

Meena was waiting for her grandson, sitting on the swing, with Ginger curled up on a cushion beside her.

"Dev," she called, as he was about to step out of the house.

"*Daadima,*" he said, changing direction and walking towards her, "I thought you were going to sleep."

She smiled, "Yes, of course, after my lunch settles down. Has Anya gone to sleep?"

"Yes, she's out like a light." A soft smile lingered on Dev's face as he thought of Anya.

"You like her."

Dev grinned at his grandmother. "You were always smart, *Daadima*. Why do you think I insisted that you come to live with me?" he said, hugging her.

Meena laughed. "Do I dream of a wedding soon?"

The smile disappeared from Dev's face. "Wedding *toh door ki baat hai*. I don't know, *Daadima*," he sighed, "Anya's suffering from memory loss. She can't recall anything from before the day she opened her eyes in the hospital. You know what that means, right? She doesn't even recognise her parents or friends or colleagues. Nothing! A lot of healing needs to happen. A life partner is the last thing she will want at this point in life."

"Oh!" Meena's eyes widened in horror, "The poor child. No wonder she doesn't smile much. It must be terrible, not remembering anything. But Dev, where is her family? Do they know that she is unwell?"

A deep sigh shuddered from Dev's wide chest. "She's an only daughter *Daadima*. Her parents know, but I'm not sure that they really care enough. Suffice to say, she's better off staying with us."

"How can you say that, Dev? They must be worried silly," said Meena in a scolding voice.

"*Daadima*, you can say that after knowing your son and daughter-in-law?" he looked at her with accusing grey eyes which had turned stormy.

Meena sighed. Her grandson was referring to his own parents. They had disowned him when he decided to become a farmer. That had been a little more than five years ago. In the last two years, *after* reading about his success stories in newspapers and magazines, Dev's parents wanted to make their peace with him. But he was too angry to care. When he bought the farm at Karjat, it was Meena who had given him her blessing and had agreed to move in with him when he requested her to. Dev had always been close to his grandmother more than his parents. His siblings—mixed twins Jai and Chaahat—were seven years younger to him. He had not got very close to them as they were comfortable in each other's company. It had always been *Daadima* he spent time with. Their family lived in Mumbai, but he had not bothered to contact any of them during his stay there the whole of last week.

Meena placed a pacifying hand on her grandson's stiff shoulder. "Not all parents are the same, Dev. What if Anya's parents love her? They must be concerned for her."

Dev gave a bitter laugh, shaking his head. "No *Daadima*, they are no different from Mom and Dad. You don't want to know." He got up suddenly. "I'll go check what's happening at the farm, *Daadima*. It has been more than a week." He waved to her and left.

14

It was a week since Anya had moved into Dev's home. She had spoken to Farhan a few times, assuring him that she was fine. Well, she was, if she did not think about her past, or rather the time of her life which was a blank canvas.

Dev's grandmother was a loving woman and treated Anya like her own granddaughter. Dev accompanied her on short walks in the evening and did his best, which was a lot, to spend time with her despite his busy schedule.

Actually, Anya felt like a princess as she was waited on hand and foot at every turn. There were six families working on the farm, who also lived in their own houses, built for them by Dev. There was also a bachelor home of sorts where twelve young men had their accommodation. The people who worked on the farm also took care of the housework. There was Seema who made the meals for the family. Her husband Dharmesh worked as a supervisor on the farm while their children went to a boarding school in Panchgani, all thanks to their boss. Anya got to know the people one by one. She learned to smile more as she created new memories which were also truly happy ones.

Just now she was at the kennel, watching Kitty feeding her three kittens. While the wooden structure was four feet tall and could comfortably house a dozen dogs, the cat had taken over the small loft which had been built into the structure for that very purpose. The little ones had just opened their eyes since that morning. Anya knelt on the floor, watching them with a smile of pure joy on her face. One, a male, was pure ginger, same as its father, she presumed. Anya called him Jupiter. She called the grey one with a white belly Venus, as it was a female and the charcoal-coloured kitten was named Mars, another male.

Dev laughed out loud when he heard the names for the first time, his teeth gleaming in the early evening sunlight. "Such big names for these tiny ones," he teased.

Anya wrinkled her nose at him. "They will grow big, won't they?!"

"I suppose you have a point there. And how did you come up with those names in the first place?" he asked curiously.

"You have such awesome books in your library, Dev. I've been catching up on a lot of reading. I hope you don't mind."

"Not at all," he shrugged. "Books are meant to be read. I should have told you about the library. It is I who am sorry that I..."

She shook her head, her hair bouncing against her flushed cheeks. "No worries there. *Daadima* showed me the room." She had actually squealed in pleasure when Meena escorted her to the library which was on the opposite side to Anya's bedroom on the first floor. Half a dozen cosy single sofas were scattered around the room while three walls were taken up by wooden shelves from floor to ceiling, crammed with books. Small labels were fixed above the shelves to let the reader know the subjects the books dealt with. While most of the books were fiction, there were some serious tomes out there too. The only free wall was a bay of floor length windows which opened into the wraparound veranda, bringing a lot of bright sunlight and a view of the lush hills.

Dev was glad to see some colour on her cheeks as he nodded. "So that's how you came up with the names of planets for those poor little kitties," he winked.

"Dev." She punched him on his arm. "Do you want me to change them?" she asked, looking up into his grey eyes. It was the first time she noticed how long his eyelashes were, appearing almost feminine.

"Of course not. I don't think they mind," he grinned, turning to stroke a gentle finger down the back of Mars. Kitty opened her eyes. Assured it was Dev who was touching her baby, she shut her eyes again.

Anya sighed softly, taking in the serene atmosphere of Kitty and her small family. Ginger had jumped on to the loft and settled beside them. Even the dogs did not bark too loudly in the area, seemingly attuned to the sleeping babies. How adorable!

"I so love it here Dev. Thank you so much for inviting me. It's just that..."

"You've already thanked me a million times, Anya. And what's bothering you now?" he asked, a dark eyebrow up in query as he studied her lovely face.

"Can I do some kind of work? I can't recall what I am trained for, even with my MBA degree and all that." She looked up at him with a bitter half smile on her face. "But I'm sure I can pull my weight around your farm, helping with the planting or harvesting or whatever your workers do."

Dev got up from his crouching position, pulling her up along with him, stroking a rough finger down her silky cheek. "I know you're anxious to help but don't forget that you are recuperating from a terrible accident. Why don't you give your body the time to heal? You have an appointment with Dr. Adnani in three days. Let's go meet him before I take you up on your offer." While he spoke softly, his tone was firm, brooking no argument.

"But Dev, I feel so useless, living the life of a lotus eater. I…" His finger on her cheek was so distracting, making it difficult for Anya to concentrate on what she was saying.

"Would you like to go around the farm with me tomorrow? I can show you how it all works. Maybe like a preliminary round so that you can find out if you would really like to work on a farm. What say?"

Anya looked into his eyes, excitement beating a soft tattoo in her heart. She so wanted to know more about Dev and his farm. "That would be lovely, Dev. Are you sure I won't get in your way?"

"I'm sure you will," said Dev, his eyes twinkling with mirth and his tongue tucked firmly in cheek, "but I wouldn't mind."

"Dev." Anya gave him a mock glare, too pleased to mind his teasing. "It's a date then. When do you want to leave?"

"Immediately after breakfast? We'll get back home for lunch so that you don't get too tired."

"I'm sure I won't," said Anya, excited at the prospect of going around the farm. She wanted to know about the farm was one thing. The other reason was that she craved to spend more time with Dev.

Anya blanched, moving her gaze to the ground. Now where the hell had that thought sprung from?!

15

Renu Gurnani walked into the Wadhwa home as if she owned the place. It was barely nine in the morning and she wanted to catch Dev before he took off to the farm. But he did not seem to be around. She would have known as the whole area vibrated with his energy whenever he was there. Noticing his grandmother sitting on the swing at the other end, Renu walked across the sunlit courtyard to meet her.

"Hello Meena *Daadi, kaisi ho?*"

"*Aao* Renu," smiled Meena, at their closest neighbour's daughter. "I'm fine. And how are you? Did you enjoy your trip to Europe?" The old lady was aware of the young woman's interest in her grandson and also knew that Dev had never eyed Renu as a prospective life partner.

"It wasn't bad, *Daadi*. Where's Dev?"

Meena looked at Renu in surprise. The woman had been to Europe with her family and had found the experience 'not bad'. How cynical was that! But then, the girl had been born with a silver spoon and never appreciated how lucky she was. Meena realised that she was being judgemental, but then, that is how she was. "Dev has gone to work," she replied.

"Already?" Renu frowned. "Isn't it too early?"

Meena smiled. "You know how Dev is, living his life exactly the way he wants." And Meena was absolutely proud of her grandson. "Actually, we have a guest staying with us. He has taken Anya to show her around." She gave her neighbour a sly look from the corner of her eyes to check her reaction to the news.

That sure stopped Renu in her tracks. "What? You have a guest? Who's Anya?" Renu was territorial and believed that Dev was her property. It never occurred to her that he might have a say in that. She thought he belonged to her and that was it. Well, Dev had never shown an interest in any woman before. Who was this new guest? Was she young or old? Beautiful or ugly? Renu was dying of curiosity.

"Anya Chhabria is from Mumbai. She has had an accident and is recuperating here at our home."

"Do you know when they will be back?" asked Renu, with a glint in her eyes.

"I'm not sure, though they will get back before lunch," said Meena, a mischievous look in her eyes. She could not wait to see the real-life drama which was sure to unfold.

Renu got up to leave. "I'm telling Seema to set one extra place for lunch, *Daadi*. I'll be back later."

Meena nodded, as Renu went in search of the cook.

Renu was fuming when she stepped out of the house after giving her instructions to Seema. Her body had gone rigid when she heard that the Wadhwas had a lady guest, someone who was staying for long. Recuperating from an accident indeed! Meena *Daadi* had not mentioned if the guest was a relative or a friend. Renu concluded that she was neither. How could Dev bring someone home just like that? What if the woman was after Dev's fortune? Renu was sure of it. The man might be handsome and a smart farmer-entrepreneur, but he was totally dumb when it came to judging women. Take herself for instance. She had been chasing him over the last five years, from the time Dev and his grandmother had purchased the neighbouring farm and settled down there. But he was completely unaware of her interest. It had not mattered till now. But Anya's advent into his life had put Renu on red alert mode. It was high time she took charge of his life. Renu got into her jeep and roared away, too angry with Dev and his guest.

Anya felt the warmth the moment she entered the poly house. Dev had driven her in the Innova Crysta for about ten minutes before they reached the first structure. It looked like a large tent. He explained that the flowering plants were grown within the structure to help maintain the correct temperature and humidity for best results.

She pulled off the V-necked, full-sleeved sweater she was wearing over a t-shirt to combat the November cold in Karjat. Pushing her hair out of her eyes, she gasped when she noticed the row upon row of plants which grew gerbera flowers. Anya did not wait for Dev as she walked in the space between the rows looking at the luxuriant blooms on the healthy green plants. The flowers were just opening and were in shades of brilliant pink, red, orange, yellow and white, the colours separated row wise. "They all look so wonderful, Dev," she called out to the man who was walking right behind her, his hands tucked into the pockets of his jeans. "What do you do with so many flowers? Do you export them?" she asked, stopping to turn and look at him.

He nodded, a broad smile on his face. "Yes, I export some of them while also selling some locally."

"I was under the impression that we imported exotic flowers into India. This is simply amazing."

He grinned. "I wonder where you got that piece of knowledge from. But you're right. We used to import some of these flowers some years ago, until we cultivated the art of growing them right here, on our soil."

"Though it all looks so beautiful, it must be a lot of work, right?"

He shrugged, drawing her eyes to his wide shoulders, the muscles rippling under his cotton shirt. "Of course, it's a lot of work. But we have enough people working here, so no one is overworked. And I think my employees are happy to work at Wadhwa Farm."

Anya nodded. That was something she had been noticing over and over again. Dev treated them all like one big family, taking care of all their requirements. She walked down the pathways, stopping to check the especially large blooms when she caught sight of a troop of women walking into the poly house.

"They have come to pluck the flowers. They will pick them colour-wise and place them in buckets of water immediately after plucking." Anya nodded, listening to him keenly. "And then they take the buckets of gerbera to the cool house to grade them as per their size. We can go to see the roses and carnations before going to the cool house to see how it operates. What say?" asked Dev.

"How many types of flowers do you grow?" asked Anya in awe.

"Six, along with the lilies, anthuriums and orchids with a few types of baby's breath thrown in. And then there is the vegetable patch where we grow all our needs, for the house as well as the workers and their families."

"I'm impressed," said Anya, untying her sweater from around her neck, to wear it on their way out.

While the carnations and lilies were awesome, it was the roses that Anya fell in love with. She realised that she could spend hours there, simply staring at them. Nets were placed around individual buds, protecting their shape. "It must be difficult to keep out the pests, nah?" she asked, quirking a shapely eyebrow at him.

"We have our methods. The advantage is more when they are in a closed environment as that keeps away most of the insects." Dev cut the long stem of a dark red rose, removing the thorns and the net before presenting it to her. "This is for you. Can you believe that this variety is called *Top Secret* in North India?"

"Thank you, Dev," said Anya, caressing the silky velvet top of the flower which was still not fully open with a dainty finger. She pressed her nose to it delicately, inhaling its perfume. "Are you saying it has another name in the South?" she asked, her smile both sensual as well as innocent as she looked up into his eyes which reminded her of the dark clouds which seemed ever prevalent around the Sahyadri mountains close to his home.

Dev felt envious of the flower as Anya played with it. He looked up into her eyes, trying to recall her question. Remembering it with an effort, he replied, "They call it the *Taj Mahal* there."

"Are you saying the roses have different names to them?" She suddenly felt tired and overwhelmed from their morning at the farm. Though they had done most of the travelling around in the station wagon, there had been so much to see.

Seeing her drooping features, Dev took her elbow in his hand. "Yes, they do. But all that for another day. Let's get you home now."

"But Dev, we haven't seen your orchids and anthuriums. And oh yes, the vegetable patch, I so want to see it," she protested.

"They aren't going anywhere. We can see them all tomorrow," he said, escorting her to the car.

"Dev." She wanted to stamp her foot in frustration, but could not find the stamina.

He stopped, looking down at her. "Anya…" He so wanted to fold her into his arms and transfer his energy into her. She looked frail just now. Had they overdone the morning sightseeing? Anya had even stopped to ask the labourers a lot of questions. And just now she looked as if she might fall down if he let go of her arm. Dev lifted her up in his arms to walk the few more steps to his car, not listening to her weak protests. He opened the passenger door and placed her on the seat, buckling the seatbelt around her. Walking around to the driver's side, he rode the car through a different route on their way back home.

"What's that?" asked Anya, sighting a large body of water.

"It's an artificial lake that I had had built, especially for the farm."

"Oh yes, you must need lots of water to keep the plants so lush and green," she nodded. "Thanks for calling a halt when you did. I'm feeling beat." Anya gave him an impish smile.

"A gentleman never says, 'I told you so'," he grinned, his teeth flashing brightly in the noon sunlight.

"Are you a gentleman?" she asked cheekily.

"That's for you to say."

She studied him from half-closed eyes, leaning against the door, before nodding slowly. "You definitely are."

She closed her eyes tiredly, not noticing the ruddy colour which suffused his manly cheeks.

16

Anya protested feebly when Dev insisted on carrying her up to her bedroom. "Please Dev…"

"Please what?" he whispered, as he walked up the staircase, holding her in his arms as delicately as if he was holding a bunch of flowers.

Dev's breath stirred the tendrils of hair which lay on Anya's cheek, making her aware of the strong, muscular arms which held her with absolute ease. He was not even a tad breathless after walking with her in his arms all the way from where he had parked the car at the portico. She opened her eyes a slit to study the sharp features which had become very dear to her in the couple of weeks she had known him. His broad forehead bespoke an intelligence that she could not help but notice at every turn. Dark grey eyes looked at her from under bushy eyebrows, their expression unfathomable. He had chiselled cheeks which met in a firm, square chin, a prominent, aquiline nose and sensual lips to die for.

Dev treated her with such love and care. Somehow, Anya was sure that no one had given her so much of themselves in all these years. Yes, she could sense that despite her memory loss. That she could not have managed without his help was for sure. A deep sigh broke free from her at the magnanimity of her situation. While the whole world appeared to be full of unknown faces to the amnesia patient, Dev was the one who grounded her.

She smiled at him now, raising a hand to touch his rough cheek. He already sported a five o'clock shadow, despite having shaved that morning before they left for their trip around the farm. "You're spoiling me," she declared.

"Looks like you could do with some spoiling," he smiled, touched by the feather light caress on his cheek. Would her lips still taste as fresh, like the other time he had kissed her? Dev could not help wondering as he laid her down on the bed and turned to take the tray from the maid who carried two tall glasses of chilled lemonade, placing it on a side table.

"I thought you might like to have some chilled lemon juice," he said, plumping the pillows behind Anya to help her sit comfortably.

Anya shook her head at him, her coffee brown gaze clinging to his gentle grey eyes. "There you go again, spoiling me rotten."

"Guilty as charged," he grinned, taking a glass and handing it to her. "Cheers!" he said, sipping from his own. If he could do it, he would wrap her in cotton wool and bury her deep within his heart.

She also drank from her glass before saying, "Why the hell do I feel so weak, Dev? I really hope I'm not one of those people who sit back on their butt throughout the day, twiddling their thumbs." She grimaced at the picture she painted of herself.

Dev threw back his head and laughed, startling her into staring at him. She ogled at the length of his strong throat, fighting the sudden, inexplicable urge to bury her face in it. Was it her imagination or did he appear handsomer than ever today?

"Farhan tells me that you passed your MBA in marketing with flying colours. I don't think that would've been possible if you were the type to sit on your butt, twiddling your thumbs," he teased.

"Tch," said Anya, her shoulders hunched, "What's the use anyway?"

Dev took the empty glass from her and placed it on the tray beside his, before lifting her chin with a thumb and forefinger. "Don't tell me you're going to give up now, my little warrior?" He raised an eyebrow that touched the silky hair which had fallen on his forehead.

"Right now, I don't feel anything like a warrior," she grumbled, grimacing. She felt frustrated by the weakness which assailed her body. Shouldn't she feel stronger after all this time?

"Anya, look at me," commanded Dev in a gentle but firm voice. When she did, he continued, "Don't be so hard on yourself. Give it time and your body will recover, for sure."

"How much more? It has been all of two weeks since the accident."

Dev could not stop himself from running his fingers through her tousled hair. "It's a matter of perception. According to Dr. Adnani, you have come a very long way in such a short time."

"Did you speak to him?" she asked, her eyes closing of their own volition as he continued to caress her head, his fingers lightly massaging her scalp.

"Every day," he said in a whisper, noticing that she was almost asleep.

"What?!" Anya opened her eyes, suddenly alert. "You've been in touch with the doctor every day?" She had not known.

Dev nodded. "He was insistent that I give him a daily report on your progress."

Where did Dev find the time to do all this? He spent so much time with her, caring for her personally, not relegating anything to the umpteen servants who worked around the house and farm. Then there was his twenty-five-acre farm and the business surrounding it. Anya looked up at him, her heart thudding loudly. He appeared like a powerhouse of energy, lighting up everything and everyone who came in his path. What had she ever done to deserve him in her life? And what would happen to her when she recovered her strength fully? She had no idea of what job she used to do before her accident. She could not recall any kind of training, nor her MBA course. What would she do? She could not depend on Dev forever.

"I'm scared Dev. I don't want to be so dependent on anyone. What if I never recover my memory?" she asked him pathetically, her eyes turbulent in her pale face.

Dev lifted her up to pull her into his arms, tucking her head in his broad shoulder, a deep sigh shuddering through him. He rubbed a large hand soothingly down her back, doing his best to calm her down. "I've been looking for someone to market my farm products. Yes, they've been selling, but I'm constantly expanding the farm. Just last month I bought five more acres. I'm thinking of getting into organic vegetables with the extra land. The veggies market will be completely new to me. Would you like to learn more about flower and vegetable farming and do the marketing for Wadhwa Farm?" he asked. He had been thinking long and hard about this. Farhan had claimed that Anya was an expert at what she did. While the industry was different, it all boiled down to finding the right buyer and convincing the person to purchase their produce. And there was no need to rush. She could learn on the job. All this long, Dev had done the work himself. But with the expansion and all that, he found his time shrinking. He definitely could do with a helping hand.

Anya raised her head to gaze up at him warily. "Are you sure you aren't creating the job for me?" she asked.

"Do I look like a foolish businessman to you?" he challenged, looking at her penetratingly.

She continued to look at him for some time, hoping against hope that he believed her capable of being his marketing person. She suddenly grinned, shaking her head. "That you are not."

"Phew! You had me worried there for a minute," he grinned teasingly. "Do you think you can come down for lunch or shall I have someone bring you a tray here?"

"I'm fine. I'll…"

"Dev," called Renu from farther away, interrupting Anya mid-sentence, making her wonder who it was.

Dev shut his eyes for a second, working at controlling his annoyed expression, before opening them. Even before he could call out an answer, Renu had appeared at the entrance to Anya's room.

"Hello Renu," he greeted her in a neutral voice. The woman popped up at his home whenever she pleased, without invitation. He never said anything as she was friendly with his grandmother and he did not want to appear rude.

"Dev, I heard you've a guest staying with you," said Renu, pouting at him. She was dressed in a short, shocking pink dress which stopped at mid-thigh, her face full of makeup despite it being barely one in the afternoon.

"Yes, meet Anya Chhabria, my guest. And Anya, this is Renu Gurnani, our neighbour," introduced Dev.

"Not just neighbour, I'm his close friend," insisted Renu, before saying, "Hello Anya." She checked the other woman from head to foot, not noticing Dev roll his eyes towards the ceiling at her back. Renu dismissed the pale Anya as no competition. Dev could not be interested in this waif when his vibrant neighbour was around. If she had entered the room all of five seconds earlier or without calling out to him, she would have been shocked to find the guest in Dev's arms.

"Hello Renu," said Anya, giving her a small smile.

"So, shall we go down for lunch?" asked Dev, "Or do you want to rest for a while?"

"Shall I be down in half an hour?" asked Anya, her eyes begging his understanding.

"Of course. We'll go down while you have a much-needed rest," he said, pointing Renu to the doorway, without touching her. That was another thing that irritated him no end, her trying to touch him at every opportunity.

Renu pouted at him, waving to Anya, before tucking her hand firmly into his elbow as they went out of Anya's room.

"What's wrong with Anya?" asked Renu, in a loud whisper.

"She had an accident," said Dev briefly, managing to extricate his arm when they reached the staircase. "Renu, you go on down. I need to make a call," he said.

"Let me wait for you," said the persistent woman.

He shook his head. "It's a business call. You'll be bored to tears." Turning away from her, he walked to the other end of the corridor, taking his phone out to call Shaan. It was only a brief call to his manager and could have waited. But Dev was only doing his best to get Renu out of his hair.

Turning towards the staircase, he was not really surprised to see her waiting right where he had left her. With a deep sigh, he walked towards her, realising that she was too tenacious. Maybe it was time to deal with her a bit more firmly.

He nodded to her before taking the stairs speedily, not giving her a chance to cling to his person. To hell with chivalry!

"*Daadima,* are you hungry or can we delay lunch by half an hour?" asked Dev, sitting next to Meena on the swing, after pulling out a chair for Renu. "Anya's a bit tired with the morning rounds, and is resting."

Meena nodded immediately. "I have no problem, Dev. The poor child! I hope the exertion hasn't set back her recovery." She looked at him with concern in her eyes.

Renu's temper simmered as the two of them conversed as if she was not around. "Meena *Daadi*, there's nothing wrong with the girl. I saw her myself," she declared, doing her best to draw their attention to herself.

Meena frowned, turning to look at Renu. "Can you please wait, Renu? I need to know something. Dev? Do you think Anya has suffered a setback?" She had noticed her grandson carrying her up the stairs a while ago.

Dev shook his head, hugging his grandmother. "No *Daadima*. She is just winded. I checked with the doctor before taking her out today. She is improving for sure, though it will take time. I thought the fresh plants and flowers will prove to be healing."

Grandma nodded with a sigh. "You are right. If you have checked with her doctor, then fine. There's nothing to worry," she smiled. Turning to Renu, she said, "*Haan* Renu, what were you saying?"

Renu looked from one to the other with venom in her eyes. "Just that your guest seemed perfectly fine to me when I met her a few minutes ago."

If Meena was angry, she did not show it, inherent manners stopping her from being rude to a guest.

But Dev was too annoyed by now. "Renu, I think you should refrain from passing judgement as you have no clue about Anya's condition. Are we agreed on that?" His tone was iron cloaked in velvet.

Catching the slowly boiling temper in Dev's stormy grey eyes, Renu decided to shut up, giving him a small nod. She felt the jealous green monster rearing its head within her as she realised that the grandmother-grandson duo was too protective of their guest. She would need to bide her time. First, she would have to find out how long Anya was planning to stay with the Wadhwas.

Anya came down in twenty minutes, feeling much better after lying down for a while. "I'm so sorry to keep you waiting, *Daadima*," she said, smiling at Meena.

"Not at all, *beta*. Did Dev make you run around too much?" asked Meena, getting up from the swing.

Anya's answering grin lit up her face, making Renu wake up to danger. "Of course not, *Daadima*. He even refused to take me to see the vegetable patch, insisting that I had already done too much for one morning."

"What vegetable patch?" piped up Renu, visibly unhappy at not being the centre of attention. "You never told me that you grew vegetables, Dev," she pouted at him.

Dev shrugged. "It's *Daadima's* pet project," he said, tongue-in-cheek, turning to give Meena a small wink.

When Renu turned to look at Meena, the old lady said, "Yes, you can say that. *Chalo*, let us have lunch. I'm famished," she said, changing the subject adroitly. While she admired her grandson for his green fingers, Meena personally could never identify a root from a shoot and did not interfere with any of the farming activities. If Dev wanted Renu to believe that the vegetable garden was his grandmother's pet project, he must have his reasons for it. Meena decided to just play along. She also could see that Renu did not like Anya's presence in Dev's life. Too bad! Meena, for one, preferred the younger woman any day. Anya had way better manners than their rude and cynical neighbour.

They chatted about this and that as they ate their way through the *paneer makhani, garlic naan* and *Hyderabadi mutton biryani* with *kachumber.*

"Thank you, Seema Aunty," said Anya, licking her fingers, "That was simply yummy. You must be the world's best cook."

Seema gave the young guest a brilliant smile, touched by the heartfelt compliment.

"I'm sure there's no need to gush," said Renu rudely, "she's only doing her work."

Anya gave the other woman a startled look. "But a compliment will surely not hurt, will it? You saw it made her so happy. I..."

"Making the servants happy isn't what we're here for, are we?" challenged Renu, looking at Dev first and then at Meena.

Anya took a deep breath to cool down her rising temper. She never knew that she could anger so fast. She looked at the other woman calmly, refusing to answer her.

Dev shrugged. "There's no doubt that Seema Aunty is the best cook ever. And thank you for telling her so, Anya," he said, raising his water glass in a toast to his guest, not addressing Renu. The woman had turned to be a thorn in his flesh, someone he needed to get rid of as soon as he could.

Hell hath no fury like a woman scorned! Neither Dev nor Anya realised the impact of their conversation on Renu Gurnani. Fuming, Renu gritted her teeth and continued to smile and chat, pretending as if nothing had happened, while the wheels turned furiously in her brain as she planned Anya's exit from Dev's life.

Anya and Dev left in the morning on Friday to keep their appointment with Dr. Adnani. This time, Dev flew the helicopter himself, surprising Anya yet again. She sat next to him, thoroughly enjoying the ride as she felt way healthier than their last outing.

Dr. Adnani was happy with Anya's physical progress. "Your wound is completely healed. No worries there. Any glimpses of your past life?" he asked gently.

Anya shook her head, her lips drooping. "Unless you count the general stuff that I can remember. Like, I can manage to use my laptop and smart phone. I know how to drive a car. But then, I also know how to walk and eat," she grumbled, a bitter smile on her face. She paused for a second, before apologising, "I'm sorry, Dr. Adnani. That was rude. Please forgive me."

Dr. Adnani shook his head. "Not at all, my dear. Do not tax yourself. You're lucky to have Dev looking out for you."

Anya sighed. "You are right, doctor. I should be thankful to have a safe haven to recuperate. Dev and his grandmother go out of their ways to take care of me. I'm truly lucky. But tell me the truth, doctor. What are the chances of my ever recovering my memory? I feel like an invalid at times." She felt so sorry for herself.

"Well, there's really no reason why you shouldn't remember your past. After speaking to your parents and your ex-husband, I don't think you underwent any mental trauma in the past. The amnesia is only due to the shock to your brain. Now that you are completely healed physically, I don't think there should be a problem with you regaining your memory." He raised a hand to stop Anya when she would have interrupted. "That said, I can't promise either a quick recovery or… let me be upfront. There have been a few cases cited around the world where patients never remembered their past lives. That again doesn't mean you cannot lead a normal life."

"How can you say that, doctor? Can you even imagine what it feels like? I can't remember a single instant of my life for twenty-four years. How can you even suggest that I might be able to lead a normal life?" Anya's brown eyes glared accusingly at the doctor.

"Listen Anya. I understand your anxiety and while I haven't experienced it firsthand, I do realise to some extent of what you must be undergoing. But you know the saying, 'what can't be cured has to be endured'. At least, you don't suffer from physical disabilities. And your mind is still active and strong. You are able to form new memories. Which is a major plus under the circumstances."

"I suppose."

"The harder you try, the further your memories might seem out of reach. Try to relax more. Have you thought of taking up a job? Something light for which you may not need too much qualification?"

Anya nodded. "I'm planning to work as marketing manager for Wadhwa Farm. I believe I've an MBA degree in marketing. Let me see if the knowledge comes to the fore."

"There's no reason why it shouldn't. This is an excellent idea. If you keep your mind occupied, chances are high that you might stop putting pressure on your brain to remember. The less pressure, the better chances of remembering. But then, it's like my telling you not to think of a monkey while taking your medication. Monkey probably will be the first thing which comes to your mind every time you take your medicine." Dr. Adnani's eyes twinkled behind his spectacles, bringing a smile to Anya's lips.

She nodded, her face less pained now, giving him a smile. "Thank you so much for your time, Dr. Adnani, and your kind words."

"Not at all, my dear. I wish you a speedy recovery." He shook her hand. "Will you ask Dev to meet me for a minute before you leave?"

"Sure doctor," said Anya, curious to know what he might have to say to Dev that the doctor did not want to utter in her presence. But well, she mentally shrugged, there was nothing she could do about it.

She stepped out of the consulting room, looking for Dev who was sitting back on a sofa, speaking on his cell phone. Seeing her, he excused himself before disconnecting the call, getting up to meet her halfway.

"Dr. Adnani would like to speak to you," she said, "Alone."

Dev grinned at her, touching her cheek reassuringly before going into the consulting room.

"Dev," greeted the doctor, a big smile on his face. "Sit down."

"And how are you Dr. Adnani?" asked Dev. He had liked the doctor from the first time he had spoken to him. His presence was calming and he never seemed to panic.

"I'm fine, Dev. About Anya. It's great that she's able to recuperate at your home and she's healing really well. But what I'm thinking is that your place is completely new to her. She didn't know it before the accident. This is just an idea and I don't know if it will really work. But it might help if she went to familiar places such as her own home in Mumbai or her office, if that's possible. Even visiting her parents in their hometown might trigger something."

Dev nodded, listening keenly. "Let me see what can be done, doctor. Just the mention of her parents seems to disturb Anya."

Dr. Adnani looked at him keenly. "There might be something there, which is all the more reason to explore. But let's give it some more time—maybe another month or two. Are you going to be in Mumbai for a while or returning immediately?"

"We were planning to return today. But tell me, doctor. What do you suggest?"

"How about revisiting her apartment and meeting her ex-husband, Farhan?"

"We are meeting Farhan for lunch. And your idea sounds practical. We'll take her to her home. I'll see what can be done."

Dr. Adnani got up, suggesting that the meeting was over. "That would be perfect, Dev. As I mentioned to Anya, she's very lucky that she has you to take care of her."

Dev smiled. "To be truthful, I'm the lucky one. I would never have wished the accident on Anya. But if that's what was required to bring us together, then I'm simply grateful that it happened."

Dr. Adnani looked into Dev's eyes to see the love shining in them and nodded, a smile on his face.

"Wish you the very best, young man."

Dev shook the doctor's hand before leaving.

"What did he say?" asked Anya, curious.

Dev draped an arm around her shoulders as they continued to walk down the hospital corridor. "That you're recovering and it might help trigger your memories by revisiting your flat. What do you say?"

Anya looked up at him, her face pale. "Let's do it. Do you know where to go?" she asked pathetically.

"That's no issue. Let's ask Farhan during lunch."

"Perfect," said Anya, while her expression suggested just the opposite.

Dev guided her to a chair at the hospital canteen. "Would you like some coffee or tea? Farhan should be here in about fifteen-twenty minutes."

Anya sprung from her chair like a jack-in-the-box, extremely restless. "You sit down Dev. And tell me what you want. I'll go get it from the self-service counter."

Dev looked at the glint in her eyes and realised she meant business. "I'll have a coffee," he said, with a calming smile on his face.

Only it did not work its charm on the angry woman. Life had been fine at Wadhwa Farm. Why the hell did they have to visit the doctor? Dr. Adnani had not been of any help in bringing her memory back and returning to the hospital had only served to trigger a lot of unpleasantness for Anya.

She took an about turn and went to the cashier to pay for two coffees before carrying the bill to the service counter. It was difficult not to howl in frustration. It was fucking twenty-four years of her life, damn it. And even that, Anya only knew because someone else had told her. She could be twenty or forty for all she knew. She lifted the paper cups and walked to the table where Dev sat, placing the coffee carefully in front of him, refusing to meet his eyes.

Dev sipped his coffee, looking at the pinched face in front of him, not uttering a word. He could see that she was in pain and controlled the sigh which threatened to burst forth from within him. How much ever he wanted to give his support to her, there was nothing he could do about helping her get back her memory. But he could see that she was better off at his home. And being employed as his marketing manager would keep her mind busy, not giving her an opportunity to dwell on her past which was as good as non-existent. Without uttering a word, he took her left hand in his, giving Anya the silent support which she seemed to need so badly.

Anya's phone rang. It was Farhan. She asked him if he had arrived before disconnecting her phone and getting up, her coffee forgotten. "Shall we go?"

They met Farhan outside the hospital gates where he waited in his car along with Arth. "Hello guys," said

Dev, with a smile, while Anya raised a perfunctory hand in greeting, no smile on her face.

Farhan got out of his car to give her a hug. "What did the doctor say, Anya?" he asked, sensitive to her foul mood.

She shrugged. "He says I'm fine." She looked up into his eyes for a second before lowering her gaze as unshed tears shimmered in them.

"Anya, baby…" Farhan held her closer, pressing her head on his shoulder. "I know I may sound inane, but this too will pass. Tell me something, how do you like living in Dev's home? If you don't like it, I…"

Anya lifted her head, shaking it vigorously. "I can't think of a better place to live in, Farhan. But again, I don't *know* of any better place, either." Her lips drooped again.

"Come on Anya. Cheer up. You aren't going to come to lunch with that sad expression, are you? I thought we were going to celebrate your recovery. Unless you think that being sad will help you remember your past," he teased, an eyebrow up in query.

Anya smiled slowly at first, before the smile widened into a grin. She punched him on his shoulder, unaware that she was doing something she always used to do when Farhan teased her. "You're right. Moping isn't going to help. And I've been making Dev's life miserable. I'd better apologise to him."

"That's my girl. Come on, let's go," he said, opening the backdoor for her.

She slid in next to Dev and took his hand in hers immediately. "I'm sorry Dev, for being such a wet blanket. And thank you for your patience. I…"

Dev hugged her, pressing a kiss to her cheek. "Forget it."

Arth smiled at her via the rear-view mirror. "So, Dev's planning a weekend party at his place and has invited both of us."

"Oh really?! That'll be awesome. I hope you've agreed."

"I was waiting for Farhan. What say you, Farhan?" asked Arth.

"Let's go Arth. Unless you have something planned otherwise."

Arth shook his head. "Nope. Then that's final. Dev." He looked at the other man through the mirror, "Thank you for the invite. We'd love to go."

"Give me a time and I'll have Shaan pick you guys up," offered Dev.

"By helicopter?" asked Farhan, turning the car and driving away, "That'll be awesome Dev. Thanks," he grinned via the mirror.

They chatted about the farm as Farhan drove them to Copper Chimney in Worli. "Dev grows flowers, tonnes of them, on the farm. But it's the vegetable plot that I love, along with the strawberry shrubs. There are tomatoes, cauliflower, cabbage, carrots, brinjal, lady's finger, ribbed gourd, green, yellow and red peppers and even herbs. They taste simply divine," said Anya, enthusiastically. "Seema Aunty is a fabulous cook. Then there are the cats and dogs. You'll love them, Farhan."

Dev looked at her with an indulgent smile on his handsome face. It was obvious that she loved life on the farm. He hoped that it was a step in the right direction, before falling in love with the owner.

"I'm sure I will. Arth's mom also has two dogs, Sunny and Sandy, just adorable," said Farhan, "Though I haven't interacted much with cats."

"Kitty and Ginger make a handsome pair. They have given birth to three adorable kittens…"

"You won't believe the names Anya has given them," teased Dev, "Jupiter, Mars and Venus."

Farhan guffawed while Arth squawked, "What?"

"Now I have to go to your farm, Dev, to make the acquaintance of these kitty planets, if nothing else."

Anya gave Farhan a mock glare, even as she punched Dev on his arm, hurting herself more than she did him. "I did offer to change the names, but Dev thinks they are perfect," she said, grinning.

"Yes, that's true. The little fur balls look like tiny planets for sure."

Arth burst out laughing, unable to stop himself.

They got out of the car, while Farhan handed the car keys to a valet and walked into the restaurant, all in high spirits.

Farhan had turned completely vegetarian after he had moved into Arth's home.

"But you are crazy about chicken," protested Anya. When the men stopped eating to stare at her, she asked, "What?"

"You remembered that I used to love eating chicken," said Farhan softly.

Anya pressed both her hands to her mouth, her eyes rounded in shock. "I did, didn't I?" she said in a whisper, turning to look at Dev who was sitting next to her. "I suppose my memory is returning, in bits and pieces."

"Exactly," said Dev, recalling the doctor's advice about getting Anya to familiar people and surroundings. It was also the reason why he had invited Farhan and his partner to spend a weekend at Wadhwa Farm.

"How are you placed after lunch, Farhan, Arth? I'd like to visit Anya's apartment with her," asked Dev.

"I can take you as I'm free the whole day," said Farhan.

"I'll take an OLA to my shop. I need to get back," said Arth.

"Do you guys plan to stay over?" asked Farhan.

"I haven't really thought about it," said Dev. "It's just that the doctor advised me to let Anya visit places from her past. I thought that the apartment would be a good place to begin with."

"You are absolutely right. And if there's no need to rush back, you should probably stay back at the flat for a day or two."

Dev nodded. "Why not? What do you say Anya?"

Anya had a worried expression on her face as she tried hard, delving into her mind to see if she remembered anything about her home from the 'other life' as she thought about her forgotten past. Wiping out her frown with an effort, she said, "Let's do it."

18

nya felt choked as her heart beat like a drum when they stood outside her apartment while Farhan dug into his pocket for the keys. Opening both the outer and the inner doors, he let her walk in first.

She took a hesitant step inside, wondering if her memories would rush back to her at that very instant. The living room looked neat and clean, though it was obviously not lived in. She took a deep breath to steady her nerves, looking around curiously at the same time. Dev had walked in right behind her, giving her his silent support, while Farhan opened the windows and the door to the balcony.

There was a two-seater sofa against a wall and two cosy single sofas placed adjacently on both sides. A few coffee tables were strewn about while a wall unit contained a flat screen TV, a music system and a bookshelf crammed with books. There were a couple of framed photographs near the TV. Anya saw that one was of Farhan and Arth and another was of herself with two other women. Nope, neither appeared familiar.

Farhan held her elbow to show her the two bedrooms. One was in a sunny orange and leaf green theme. "This one is your bedroom." The bed was big enough to accommodate four people, piled up with pillows and cushions. There was a wardrobe and a dressing table with a few items of makeup, but nothing which brought forth a flicker of memory.

The other bedroom was in stark black and white. "This one used to be mine," said Farhan, a smile on his face.

She looked up at him, "Not anymore?"

Farhan shrugged. "I live with Arth at his home. Let me rephrase that before he kills me," he grinned. "We live together in our bungalow at Versova."

Anya smiled at him companionably as they walked back to the hall. In the meanwhile, Dev had switched on the refrigerator in the kitchen and put back the veggies, eggs and meat they had bought at a nearby food chain, along with some provisions, enough to last them for a few days. He had switched the kettle on and was spooning instant coffee into three mugs.

Anya was surprised that Dev knew his way around a kitchen, what with so many people to do his bidding at his farm. Was she glad to have the man on her side! "Thank you, Dev," she said softly, her eyes glowing up at him, a slow excitement bubbling within her when she realised they would be alone at the apartment that night.

Farhan got up the moment they finished their coffee, carrying the mugs to the kitchen and rinsing them at the sink. He came out and said, "I'll be off then. Will there be anything else you'll be needing? What about a change of clothes for you Dev?" he asked. "Would you like me to buy something?"

Dev shook his head, pointing to the backpack which he had left on a table. "I have all I need."

"Okay then." Farhan hugged Anya before shaking Dev's hand. "I'll be in touch. The house keys are up there," he pointed to a small shelf on the wall unit. "See you guys."

After the door shut behind him, Dev said, "I'm sure you'd like to rest for a while."

Suddenly feeling beat after their hectic day, Anya nodded. "Yes, please. I'm sorry to be such a poor hostess, Dev," she said, giving him a weak smile. "Will you be okay? I…"

Dev laughed, getting up to give her a hug. "You go on. I'll be absolutely fine. I'm carrying my work along with me."

She nodded again, stepping into her bedroom, leaving the door ajar. She opened the wardrobe to find a pair of pyjamas and t-shirt. Changing in the bathroom, she crashed on the bed, going to sleep almost immediately. She was totally out to the world when Dev checked on her a few minutes later, pulling a comforter over her and tucking her in. He could not resist pressing his lips to her left cheek, smiling when she mumbled in her sleep, something that sounded like 'Dev'. Well, a man could live in hope.

It was past eight when Anya woke up to the muffled sounds of someone reading the news on TV. She went to the bathroom to splash water in her eyes, becoming wide awake. Wiping her face and brushing her hair, she stepped into the hall to see Dev lounging on the sofa, watching TV.

"Hey," he called out with a smile on seeing her, "Come and sit down," he patted the sofa next to him.

She went and sat next to him, snuggling against his shoulder. "You smell good. Did you just have a bath?" she asked.

"Yes," he said, his arm snaking around her narrow waist, pulling her closer. He did wonder how he was going to get through the night staying alone in the apartment with only the desirable Anya for company.

Anya sat with him for a few minutes before getting up. "I'm hungry Dev and so must you be. Let me see what I can put together. I wonder if I used to cook..."

Dev got up too. "Don't worry for tonight. I already have dinner ready," he said, walking towards the kitchen.

"What? You can cook?" she asked, astounded.

Dev stopped in his tracks to look at her, a bushy eyebrow up in query. "What's so surprising about that?" he asked, grinning.

"You have so many people waiting on you, hand and foot, at the farm. I was even surprised that you could make instant coffee, actually."

Dev laughed. "What you see on the farm is a different life. I have my work that doesn't leave me time to make my own meals. Seema Aunty has the skills and she needs the remuneration, same as with all my other employees. It works for all of us as we play to our strengths. But as for me, I refuse to be dependent on others to get my things done. If that makes me arrogant, well, that's what I am."

Anya looked at him in awe. "Arrogant? From which angle?" she asked, walking with him to the kitchen. She stopped to draw in a deep breath, closing her eyes to concentrate. "You have made *Rawas fish curry* Sindhi style along with *basmati chawal*. Oh yum! Shall I make some salad to go with it?"

"I hope you don't mind, but I sliced a cucumber and tomato. Then there's *pineapple raita* which I've left in the fridge."

"Oh Dev, you've been so busy while I've been sleeping the evening away," said Anya, feeling terribly guilty.

"Why don't you do the washing up after dinner?" he offered.

Her eyes lit up. "Done."

"That's my girl. Come now, do you want to take all the food out to the hall or shall we serve our plates from here?"

"Let's serve our plates and take them over." Without thinking, she lifted a hand to open an overhead cupboard to remove two plates. She opened the drawer on the right, under the kitchen platform to remove a few bowls before opening the middle one to take out spoons and forks. Dev watched in fascination as she did not hesitate even once, going about it as if she had been doing it for a long time, which she must obviously have been. The human mind was truly amazing, with so much information buried in the subconscious. He was glad that he had acted upon Dr. Adnani's advice.

He served the *raita* in two cups and the *fish curry* in a couple of larger bowls. Serving the rice on the plates, he placed the lot on a tray, taking it to the living room.

Anya followed him with the salad, salt pepper shakers and cutlery.

"Would you like to watch a movie?" he asked.

"Bollywood? Yes, please."

Dev connected his phone to the TV and they watched *Baby*, an Akshay Kumar thriller, through the Hotstar app.

They ate their way through the food, polishing everything off. "You cook almost as well as Seema Aunty," said Anya, grinning at him.

He bowed his head in acknowledgement, smiling at her rapt face before turning his attention back to the film.

Half an hour into the movie, Anya said quietly, "I've seen this film before."

Dev paused the film using the remote and turned to give her his complete attention. "You remember seeing it?"

She looked at him, her face pale, nodding slowly. "I can remember every scene as it unfolds. But if you ask me where I watched it or who I went with," she shook her head, "I can't recall anything. If you want me to tell you what happens in the movie after some time," she shook her head again, "I have no answer to that either. What do you think? Am I making any progress or is it all just wishful thinking on my part?" she asked him pathetically.

Dev looked into her shadowed brown eyes keenly. "No, it's not wishful thinking. You are able to recall in bits and pieces. You removed the plates, cups, and spoons from their drawers without pausing to even think for a second."

"What?" Anya jumped up from the sofa, her eyes wide in astonishment. "Dev, I... oh my God! You're right. I opened the correct shelves and drawers and just took them out, didn't I?"

He got up too, hugging her. "So there you are, sweetheart. It's taking time, but your memory is coming back."

"Oh Dev, I so hope you're right," she said, burying her face in his chest.

"I know I am," he said, crossing his fingers surreptitiously. "Anya…"

She lifted her face to look up at him, her eyes damp with unshed tears.

"Don't sweetheart." He pressed his lips to the corner of her mouth. "Please don't hurt so."

Anya raised a finger to touch her lips, giving him an odd look.

"What?" asked Dev.

She shook her head at him. For a second there, his lips on hers had seemed familiar. Anya gave a mental shrug. It was probably wishful thinking on her part.

They watched the film till the end, arguing amiably about the story and acting.

"Would you like to have some green tea?" asked Anya.

"We didn't buy any," said Dev.

"But there's always some stock in my kitchen," said Anya, giving him a small wink. "Yes, that's another thing which I recalled. Sudden pictures flash in my mind, like the teabags just now."

He nodded, following her into the kitchen. She switched on the kettle and washed the vessels efficiently. "The teabags are there, on that shelf," she pointed, even as Dev removed a couple of mugs.

He made the green tea and they carried their mugs to the living room.

Anya sipped at hers, her brown eyes watching him intensely. "Dev…"

"Hmm." He looked at her, his grey gaze holding hers with equal intensity.

"I…" She placed the half-drunk tea on a table before scooting closer to him.

Dev kept his mug away too, meeting her halfway. "Sweetheart," he whispered, his forefinger tracing the line of her oval face in a gentle caress. When her lips trembled in response, he pressed a kiss to the corner of her mouth and was startled when he felt her tongue peep out to trace the shape of his lower lip. Groaning, he gathered her in his arms, giving in to temptation.

Anya slicked a damp tongue over the outline of his lips, loving his masculine taste, before nipping his lower lip. She smiled when she heard him groan again. Her smile disappeared when she felt the thrust of his tongue, seeking entry into her mouth. She let him in with a moan and was excited beyond measure when he explored the contours of her mouth. She tangled her tongue with his, enjoying the sensation, her hands running through his hair, pulling his head closer. Her breasts felt heavy even as her nipples turned into hard pebbles, thrusting into his unyielding chest. She mewled like a kitten, rubbing her body against his, revelling in the contrasting textures.

Dev lifted his head to look at the woman in his arms, her head thrown back and her eyes closed, her long, curling eyelashes resting on her flushed cheeks. He bent down to trace a damp tongue on the pulse beating wildly at her throat, the same one which had not been as strong on the day of the accident. He traced the line of her graceful throat with his lips before moving down further. Holding her close with his left arm, he stroked the length of her back with his right hand, his left hand curving on her slender hip before lifting her on to his lap.

Anya clung to him, raining kisses wherever she could reach, her hands restless on his back. "Can you please get this damn shirt off?" she complained, pulling the tails out of his tailored shorts.

Dev laughed, backing away to oblige her. He did not bother to remove the buttons as he pulled the shirt off his body.

Anya stared at his wide chest, her brown eyes shining with excitement. She reached out her left hand to hold on to his muscular shoulder, her right hand running on the hair-roughened skin with relish. Colour ran up both their cheeks as Anya pressed her lips to the centre of his chest. "Dev, you are smashingly handsome," declared Anya.

"Thanks for the compliment. I want to see you, and touch you too," he said, his voice rough with passion.

She gave him a wink. "Thought you'd never ask," she said, pulling her t-shirt off.

Dev held her arms down with his hands, staring at her lace covered breasts. While her body was slim to the point of being thin, her breasts were lush, straining against the lace. Right now, they heaved as her breath deepened. "Allow me," he said, letting go of her arms to unhook her bra and flinging it on their shirts. "Anya…" he moaned, "You have such gorgeous breasts." He pressed the tip of his right thumb to a taut nipple, making Anya groan with want. He moved his thumb in a circular motion, watching the other nipple tightening further in response. Removing his thumb, he bent down to touch the tip with his tongue, flicking it gently, drawing away immediately.

"Dev!" protested Anya, her hands in his silky hair, doing her best to hold him against her. He was wreaking havoc with her body.

He smiled, grazing his teeth over the tip, his left hand cupping her right breast.

"Oh yes," moaned Anya, thrusting her breast into his palm, "Please don't stop. That feels so good."

Moulding one breast with his palm, Dev opened his mouth to take the tip of the other breast into his mouth, suckling on it gently. Anya's body went taut in his arms as she almost jumped off his lap in excitement. He opened his mouth wider and suckled harder, making her moan longer and louder.

Anya protested when he lifted his head. "No… please don't stop Dev."

"I'm going nowhere, sweetheart," he whispered in her ear, turning his head to give the same attention to the other breast. His right hand cupped her left breast which was damp from his caresses, his rough palm rubbing against the wet and engorged tip.

"Dev," whimpered Anya, thoroughly aroused by his mouth and hands on her body. Her hands caressed the rippling muscles on his back which were sheathed by satiny skin, her palms revelling in the texture. When he bit a nipple, her claws came out, raking his back, even as she moaned in desire. "I want you Dev."

"I want you too, sweetheart," he said, "Your room or mine?" he asked, lifting his head to look at her. His manhood throbbed with the need to dive into her.

"Huh?!" She opened her eyes to look up at him, surprised to see an expression akin to pain on his face. "What? Are you hurt?"

He gave her a weak grin. "Not really." He took her hand and placed it against his shaft. "Feel it?" When she nodded slowly, he grunted, "I want to get inside you, like now."

Her eyes widened in surprise even as her hand caressed his bulging manhood. He was huge!

Dev got off the sofa to lift her in his arms and took the decision out of her hands as he walked towards her bedroom. He stopped midstride with a sudden jerk. "Anya?"

She stopped nibbling his shoulder to open slumberous eyes to look at him. "What?"

"Do you have a boyfriend?"

It was as if a light had been suddenly switched off. The passion disappeared from her eyes to be replaced by utter bafflement. She shoved him away, getting out of his arms to stand on trembling feet. "How the hell would I know?" She glared at him. What lousy timing!

"I'm sorry Anya, but…"

She punched him hard on his chest, hurting herself more than him when her fists connected with his highly honed muscles. When he would have taken her hands in his, she took a couple of steps back, before turning away from him. "I hate you, Dev. Do you hear me? I hate you," she said in a loud whisper, rocking back and forth on her heels, her arms hugging her body. When she felt him move towards her, she ordered, "Don't touch me." Quickly grabbing her discarded bra and t-shirt, she held them both protectively in front of her, walking into her bedroom and shutting the door with a bang.

Dev stared at the closed door, his mind in a turmoil. Anya had been his for the taking. He did not really know what had prompted him to ask her if she had a boyfriend. While it would have been great if he had not thought of asking her the question, he realised that he wanted to know the answer. What if she regretted making love with him, once her memories returned? And return they will. He was confident of that. He fell back on the sofa, taking his cell to send Farhan a WhatsApp message. If there was anyone who would know if Anya had been in a relationship before her accident, it was Farhan.

Anya also sent a similar message to Farhan. "Do I, no… did I have a boyfriend?"

It was past midnight and Farhan did not see either of the messages till morning. Neither Dev nor Anya slept that night.

nya's phone pinged at 7 am, waking her up from the light slumber she had slid into barely an hour ago. She stretched her arm to see who it was. It was Farhan's reply to her message. "Nope, you have no boyfriend."

She got up with a jerk to sit against the headboard, slapping her phone angrily down on the pillow beside her. Her awakened body wanted to heap abuse on Dev's head. Why the hell did he have to stop midway to question her about a boyfriend? Wasn't it simple logic that if she had one, the guy would have come in search of her by now? Well, that had become clear *after* receiving Farhan's reply, but not last night. Last night, her temper had flared up fierily as she had been desperate for Dev to make love to her.

So why not now? Anya put her feet on the floor when the thought sprang forth in her mind, a small smile on her lips. They had not known if she was in a relationship last night. But now she knew differently.

Dev had given her so much of himself. Couldn't she let go of her ego and tell him what she had found out just now?

She got up immediately and went to the bathroom to wash her face and brush her hair. She had removed her pyjama bottoms before going to bed, just having pulled the t-shirt over her head. She walked out of the bedroom and went to the other one before she had a change of mind. Without bothering to knock on the door, she twisted the handle and went inside.

She stood just inside the door, watching Dev lying there, sprawled on his chest, one arm flung out on a pillow beside him. His back was bare while a thin sheet covered his lower body. She could not help staring at his snug butt which lured her closer to the bed. It was now or never. She lifted his arm slowly and slid under it, snuggling close to him.

"Anya?" mumbled Dev, turning around groggily. He had gone to sleep barely a couple of hours ago, working on his company accounts till 5 am.

"Go to sleep Dev. You must be beat if you had as bad a night as I," she whispered, her lips brushing his ear.

He promptly buried his face in her breasts, twisting a bit before he got comfortable. He was fast asleep within a few seconds.

Anya wrapped her arms around his neck, holding him close to her body, shutting her eyes with a smile on her lips, wondering if sleep would claim her. It was not long before her breathing turned even and she caught up on lost sleep.

It was past ten when Dev came awake, pressing his head into the pillow which was too comfortable for words. Wait a minute! The said pillow was breathing. He opened his eyes a slit to find that he was lying on Anya's chest as he recognised her t-shirt from the night before. What was she doing in his bed? She must have come here only in the morning as he had been awake till at least 5.30 am.

But that did not stop him from concluding that it was simply awesome waking up in her arms, his manhood springing to attention. She held him close, her arms wrapped around his back. Without his volition, Dev's hand moved low to touch the back of her bare thigh, caressing the soft skin as he continued to move further up, to press a palm to her rounded bottom. He was startled to find naked skin, his erection becoming painfully harder in response. The minx had done away with her panties. What had she been thinking, sneaking into his bed with no underclothes? He was sure she was not wearing a bra either.

A sudden thought struck him. Farhan must have replied to his message. He tried to turn around towards his phone, only to have her slender arms lock tighter around him, refusing to let go.

"Don't go away Dev," said Anya in a sleepy whisper. "I've no boyfriend. Please make love to me, I need you so much."

Dev stopped moving to look up at her, his chin pressed to the middle of her chest. Her eyes were open a slit as she stared at him. "How do you know?" he asked.

Her coffee brown eyes opened wider, sleep vanishing from them to be replaced by desire. "I asked Farhan last night. He sent me his reply today morning."

And that was why she had come to his bed. Dev smiled, his grey eyes turning smoky with passion.

He pulled her head towards his, kissing her deeply, his big hands pushing her t-shirt out of the way as he stroked her slender back. "I want you, Anya."

"I want you too," she said, moving her torso away to pull her t-shirt off.

His gaze turned tender when he saw the red marks on her breasts, the result of his lovemaking from last night. He touched a red spot gently, asking, "Does it hurt?"

She shook her head shyly, her eyes clinging to his. "Not much. My body craves for your touch."

He grinned, bending down to run his tongue soothingly over the red spots, arousing her to a fever pitch.

She turned restlessly in his arms, "Dev, I..."

He raised his head to look down at her. "Tell me what you want."

She took his hand and placed it against her feminine mound, her legs crossing to hold his hand in place. "I'm not sure," she said innocently.

He wondered if she was a virgin. Well, that was one question only she could answer, *when* she remembered. He gently parted her legs, pressing his thumb to her wetness, exploring gently, bringing forth moans from her lips. When he saw that she was ready, he moved on top of her after slipping on a condom, lifting her leg to wrap it around his waist. "This may hurt, sweetheart. But I promise to be as gentle as possible," he said, looking deeply into her eyes.

She nodded, trusting him completely. Though, that did not stop her from letting out a shriek when he entered her, her eyes going wide before shutting down.

Dev stopped, gritting his teeth, poised on top of her, afraid to move in case he hurt her more. He waited for her breathing to settle down before asking, "Do you still hurt?"

"I don't think so. Can you make it better?" she asked, looking up at him curiously. Despite the pain, her body still craved him, her feminine core throbbing with need.

Dev stirred in her arms, pulling out only to thrust again, doing his best to be as gentle as possible.

"Dev," she groaned, her nails digging into his back, her legs locking tightly around his waist.

That was all the encouragement he needed before he pounded into her, sweat gathering on his forehead despite the air-conditioner running full blast. He ran a tongue over her swollen nipples, careful not to hurt her sensitive breasts.

Anya wallowed in his thrusts, meeting him halfway, reaching out to the skies. She could feel the build up of pleasure in the depth of her womb, her body seeking utopia. Suddenly, she exploded, the orgasm catching her unawares as she sunk her teeth into his shoulder, her body rocking with unfamiliar sensations.

Dev continued to pound into her, the bite on his shoulder egging him on, before he came as he had never come before. His breath coming in gasps, Dev fell at her side, careful not to crush her with his weight, though his lower body was still joined to hers.

It was a long while before either of them could move. Dev shifted to pull her close into his arms. "Sweetheart, did I hurt you badly?"

Anya looked up at him with an impish smile on her face. "If that was hurting, please hurt me some more," she declared, pressing her soft lips to his rough cheek. "That was just amazing Dev. And no, I can't recall any experience I've had that was similar to this. And yes, I would have remembered, just like I recalled the film."

He grinned at the gorgeous woman in his arms, mighty chuffed at her compliment. Yes, Dev had fallen for Anya all over again, this time in love.

# 21

Dev and Anya got back to Karjat on Monday morning after spending a decadent weekend in Anya's apartment, making love most of their waking hours. This was the happiest Anya had been since her accident. And now she was really looking forward to working for Dev.

They shifted from the helicopter to the station wagon waiting for them. "Anya, I forgot to mention, what with the weekend being so distracting, I..."

Anya cupped Dev's cheek, smiling into his grinning face. "Did you have fun?"

"Too much," he said, giving her a wink. "After the weekend party, will you visit your parents?"

Anya frowned, removing her hand. "No Dev, unless you want to be rid of me. I was going to begin working in your farm office. Don't you want me to do that anymore?"

"Of course, I want you to. The job's waiting for you. I just want to follow Dr. Adnani's advice. You know the reason why we spent the weekend at your apartment—to help trigger your memory, if possible..."

"Oh!" She looked at him mischievously, "Pardon me if I misunderstood your intentions." She winked at him.

Dev laughed softly. "Don't get me wrong, they were the best two days of my life," he said in a whisper. He was glad it was another worker from the farm and not Ramu *kaka* who had come to pick them up from the helipad. Otherwise, they would have been inundated with questions.

She grinned at him, her eyes crinkling at the corners, pressing her hand on his thigh suggestively. "Please Dev, give me a couple of more months. Maybe then I would be ready to face those two people who are supposedly my parents." She still got disturbed whenever she thought of their hospital visit.

Dev looked at her beseeching expression and nodded slowly. "If you're sure... personally, I don't much care for the idea of your doing anything that you don't want to do. But..."

"That's my man," she said, moving her face closer to the front seat, away from the driver's purview of vision and turning towards Dev to blow him a kiss.

Anya jumped out of the car when they arrived, thrilled to be greeted by all four dogs. She could not wait to go inside the house that she had come to think of as home. And she had so missed *Daadima*.

She chatted with Meena, telling her about their visit to the doctor and about the weekend party which Dev was planning.

Meena saw Anya's glowing face and Dev's cat-that's-got-the-cream expression and drew her own conclusions, portraying only an affectionate smile on her face.

Noticing movement in one of the ceramic pots in the courtyard, Anya turned to see the three little kittens, lying on top of one another, fast asleep in the sunlight. "Oh my God!" She went to them and ran a finger over Jupiter's ginger fur as he lay on top of the other two. Stretching and yawning, he opened sleepy eyes and meowed at Anya, much to her delight. "Jupiter, you've grown up so much in the last three days," she cooed, lifting him gently in her hand. He crawled up her arm and settled in the crook of her elbow. Her eyes shining with delight, Anya turned to show her prized possession to Dev. "Isn't he the cutest?"

"Don't," teased Dev in a whisper, "You'll make Mars and Venus jealous." Those two had not moved an inch, continuing to sleep.

Anya pouted at him, "Very funny."

"I'm leaving for the farm in fifteen minutes. Do you want to go?" he asked.

"Oh yes!" She left Jupiter in the ceramic pot along with his siblings.

"Let's find out if you can ride a bicycle," said Dev mysteriously, going with her to the garage.

"Eh?" Anya looked at him curiously, wondering what he meant.

"We have half a dozen cycles and use them to get around the farm. I generally cycle to the other side of the property. You see if you can manage. If not, we'll take the car. What say?"

"That's a damn good idea, cycling around the property. So much less pollution. I'm sure I'll be able to manage." She tested the bicycle he offered her, finding it pretty comfortable. Pedalling a couple of rounds, she nodded her head. "I think I'm good."

"Just a minute." Dev took out a brilliant red cycling helmet from one of the shelves in the garage and strapped it on her head. "Now you're good to go," he said, strapping a blue one on his own.

They cycled their way to the office which was closer to the poly houses. It was a single-storied structure with a tiled roof that had one big square room with a kitchenette at the back. There was a large, rectangular desk with a leather-backed chair and a work station which could seat four. "Hello Shaan," called out Dev as they entered the office. Turning to Anya, he said, "I don't have many office staff. It's just Shaan, myself and now you. Shaan knows as much as I do about the operation and you can refer to him if you can't reach me."

Anya nodded, excited that she would finally be doing something useful. "Hello Shaan," she greeted Dev's manager.

"Hello ma'am," said Shaan, with a broad smile on his face.

"Please call me Anya," she insisted.

Dev sat with her and showed her where he kept his files. "Shaan, forward all marketing mails to Anya. Let her go through them. And also explain to her how the whole operation works—from farm to cool house to trade centre to end consumer. Anya, you get familiar with everything and let us maybe have a meeting on Wednesday morning. Does that work for you?"

Anya nodded enthusiastically. "Yes sir, it does," she said with a mischievous look on her face.

"I'll be seeing you then," said Dev, getting up from his chair. He walked close to her to give her breast a hard squeeze when Shaan turned towards his workstation to pick up his laptop. "That's for being cheeky," he told Anya.

She held his hand, a naughty grin on her face. "You're tempting me to be cheeky all the time." Her eyes dancing, Anya added after an afterthought, "Sir!"

"I'll get you for that," he promised, walking towards the door.

"I hope that's a promise," she called out to his retreating back.

Dev stepped out of the door to blow her a kiss before going on his way.

Anya was surprised when Dev walked back into the office at 1.30 pm. "Time to go for lunch," he said, "I'm famished."

"Is it that late already?" asked Anya, flexing her fingers. She had been furiously typing on her laptop, making points for the meeting on Wednesday, referring to the notes she had made when Shaan explained the workings of the farm. There was a lot to learn, but she wanted to get the morning's work in perspective before they went further.

"Yep. Are you ready to go?"

"I suppose," she said, getting up. "And Shaan?"

"He has lunch with everyone else at the community kitchen. I'll take you there one of these days. It's like a picnic," promised Dev.

"Can't we do it every day?" asked Anya curiously. She noticed that Dev treated all his workers like his own family.

"I'm sure they feel freer without me breathing down their necks all the time," he grinned.

"You've got a point there. And *Daadima* must be waiting lunch for us."

"Exactly, along with our dogs and cats," he grinned. "Here, let me help you." Dev squeezed her bottom in the pretext of helping her on to the bike.

"So, it's going to be like that," she said, looking up into his simmering hot grey eyes.

"Like what?" he asked, an innocent expression on his face.

Straddling the bike, she raised a hand to open the top button on his shirt, before reaching over to press her lips to the V, her damp tongue drawing a circle on his skin. "Hmm, you taste so good that I wouldn't mind having you for my lunch."

"Anya." Dev's voice turned guttural, his manhood making its presence felt.

"What?" Anya placed a hand against his erection, her eyes turning to molten chocolate. "Do you want me?"

"And how!" He bent down to kiss her hard, not giving a damn if anyone was watching them. She was so sinfully tempting. He gently removed her hand. "So, do I have an appointment with you tonight?"

"You bet," she whispered against his throat. "Unless *Daadima*…"

"*Daadima's* bedroom is on the ground floor. It's just the two of us on the first," he said, his hand caressing her waist, pushing her t-shirt out of the way.

"It's a date then," she said, kissing him one more time before they set off towards the main house.

They fell into a comfortable routine, Anya learning the ropes of the business. Dev accepted most of her marketing plans and gave her a free rein to go ahead in executing them. Their nights were steamy. Dev went to her bedroom on most nights as he always woke up at dawn and managed to shift to his own room by the time the servants came in. Anya found this frustrating at times, but then, they did not have a choice.

Weekends were fun at the farm. They watched a movie or two in the open air, all the families coming together. Dinner was cooked on a barbeque while *parathas* with varied fillings were made on the *tandoor* which Dharmesh set up. Everyone who knew how to cook pitched in, and they all had a gala time.

The coming weekend was to be even more entertaining with a houseful of guests. There were ten more people other than Farhan and Arth. Some of them were farmers from Mahabaleshwar while there were two couples who had gone to college with Dev.

The farm took on a festive air. Even Renu and her parents were invited for dinner on Saturday.

Renu was on her best behaviour and she really had to work hard at it as it was the most unnatural thing for her. While everyone turned up in casual clothes, she wore a short black dress with layers of makeup. The rest of the party was too well-mannered to say anything.

"Dev," she spoke in a loud whisper, "Don't you think there is something strange about Anya's friends from Mumbai? Are you aware that "both the guys" are too much into each other?" she asked, making quotation marks in the air.

Dev turned from the makeshift bar to look at her, his face stony. "So?"

"I'm just saying. I think they are gay," she continued to speak in a whisper that could be heard by at least a dozen people near them.

Dev asked again, "So?"

"*Arre*, so nothing. What is it to me? They are your guests," snarled Renu, her temper getting steadily out of control by his indifferent stance. Her hatred towards Anya had doubled, trebled, and quadrupled since the evening began. For one thing, the younger girl was dressed in a pair of snug fitting jeans and a sleeveless red *kurti* which made her skin glow. For another, Renu noticed that Dev's eyes followed Anya everywhere, as if an invisible thread connected the two.

"Exactly," said Dev, moving away in the pretext of talking to someone. He kept walking, stopping to speak to everyone, but striking a steady path towards the woman he loved. She stood out like a beacon, her smile lighting up the night. Anya made a perfect hostess, making everyone comfortable. Even his workers had taken to her and had all become her loyal fans. Dev finally reached her side. "Here you go," he said, handing her a glass of chilled wine. "Cheers!"

"Cheers!" she whispered, touching her glass to his, looking deeply into his eyes as she sipped from it. Working on his farm had given her a purpose in life, to the point that she really did not care if she remembered her life before the accident or not. Her life seemed complete with a career which gave her satisfaction and a lover who worshipped her. A home, an adoring grandmother and a houseful of pets were all an added bonus.

Farhan and Arth walked towards them. They had arrived that morning in Dev's helicopter, along with four others who were also travelling from Mumbai. "You have a fantastic set up here, Dev," said Arth, "It's amazing how you've worked singlehandedly towards achieving your dream." He was all admiration.

"And Anya, are you happy with your new job?" asked Farhan, pulling her into a hug.

"I love it," said Anya, resting her head on his shoulder. "I'm so lucky to have Dev by my side."

Renu walked towards them and caught the tail end of the conversation, losing it completely. "I'd advise you not to get too complacent. Luck tends to run out on everyone, most unexpectedly at times," she said spitefully, her eyes spouting venom at Anya. If looks could kill, Anya would have fallen dead then and there. How dare she! On the one side, she was getting too close to Dev. On the other, she was snuggling close to that gay friend of hers. Renu shook with temper. And that stupid Dev, did not he have eyes in his head? Couldn't he see that his favourite guest was playing with all men and was utterly shameless? She gritted her teeth, finding it difficult to calm down.

The ever-polite Arth turned to Renu and asked, "Would you like something to drink, ma'am?"

"I don't drink," she bit out at him.

Arth gave her a benign smile. "Maybe a soft drink?"

Dev could not help grinning despite his anger towards Renu's terrible manners. With his very politeness, Arth was underlining her rudeness and stupidity, without even meaning to.

"Dev will get one for me. He knows what my favourite is," insisted Renu, fluttering her eyelashes at him.

Arth was anything but a pushover. He bowed to Renu, saying, "I must insist. Dev has had a long and difficult day and has just stopped for a breather. Go on, tell me what your favourite is?"

Glaring at all four of them, Renu mumbled, "I don't want anything," and flounced away.

"Why is she so angry?" asked Anya, not realising that Renu was jealous of her.

Dev grinned, sitting down on a chair and pulling her down to his lap. "She probably ate something that didn't suit her."

Farhan and Arth laughed, settling on the chairs beside Dev. "You are such an innocent baby," said Farhan, "Don't ever change," he insisted.

"Yes, please don't ever," whispered Dev, nuzzling her neck.

Most of the guests left on Sunday evening while Farhan and Arth decided to leave early Monday morning. They were going to take the scenic route from Karjat, having hired a taxi, refusing Dev's offer of his station wagon and a driver.

"We had a wonderful time," said Farhan, shaking hands with Dev.

"You must stay with us the next time you are in Mumbai," insisted Arth.

They hugged Anya in turn, taking their leave, waving to them as their taxi took off.

"Shall we get to work?" asked Anya, looking at Dev.

"Slave driver," grumbled Dev, falling in step with her.

22

Two months had gone. Dev was happy with Anya's marketing tactics as they had made his products reach high end customers, cutting away the middlemen. While Dev had had two five-star hotels on his direct customer list, she had added half a dozen more by now. She had come up with social media plans and they had hired a couple of college students from Mumbai to work remotely on those.

Anya had also insisted on using the office space for a couple of hours in the evenings to teach the workers to read and write. To begin with, there were a handful of people who attended her classes. Some of them even grumbled that they did not want to spend their free time studying—not at their age. But soon, more and more joined the class until all of them were enrolled. She never gave them home work. Whatever they did, they did in the classroom. That way, there was less cause for complaint.

"You know Dev, I think we should encourage their children to take up vocational training during their holidays. It'd be great if we can organise some workshops. It will motivate them to return to the farm as well as set them up for life. What do you think?" she asked, her left hand tracing the contours of his muscular chest. They were in bed after a bout of energetic lovemaking, Dev holding her close with his left arm around her body, his eyes half closed in slumber.

"I think you're the best thing that happened to me," he said, pressing his lips to the top of her head. "You go ahead and give me a plan and budget and I'll work it in."

"I think I'm falling in love with you, Dev," she declared.

Dev got up with a jerk and sat against the headboard, pulling her up into his arms. "Tell me again."

"I am in love with you," she said, kissing his rough cheek.

"I've been waiting to hear that since forever," he said, his grey eyes aglow with adoration. "I love you too Anya. Will you marry me?"

"Hmm." She looked into his eyes. "Do you think the time has come for me to visit my parents?"

"You didn't answer my question," he said, his face shadowing with disappointment.

"I'm sorry Dev. But I still don't feel one hundred percent complete. I avoid thinking of my past most of the time. But when it comes to a life changing decision, I feel scared. Are you able to relate to what I am saying?" Her chocolate gaze begged him to understand.

A deep sigh shook Dev's frame. "The trouble is that I do, even if I don't want to. You go ahead and visit your parents as that needs to be done. But what happens in case you don't remember, even after that? Will you still refuse to marry me?" he asked.

"Even now, I'm not refusing to marry you Dev. If there's one person on earth who I want to be my partner, it's you. I…"

Dev swooped down to kiss her hard on her lips. "That's good enough for me. So, when do you want to go? I can come with you; in case you need moral support."

Anya shook her head, gently. "You've done too much Dev. I think I need to do this by myself." More than anything, she did not want Dev to be hurt just in case her parents were rude and they had seemed capable of it from what she recalled from her experience with them at the hospital. "Maybe I need to go with Farhan, if he's ready to go with me. They still don't know we are divorced," she grimaced.

Dev was not too happy with the idea, but what she said made sense. And despite her amnesia and all that, Anya was an independent woman, which was something he truly admired in her.

Dev pushed her down on the bed and went on top of her. "That's an idea," he sighed, continuing, "I've found you after so long, Anya. I don't want you to disappear from my life, ever again."

She looked at him curiously. Had he been searching for her? She shook her head to herself, assuming that she was reading more than what the situation warranted.

She called Farhan the next day. "I think it's time to face my parents, Farhan. Will you go with me? They think that we are still married. I…"

"Of course, I will. Give me a couple of days. Will check with them and also set my business in order so that I can take some time off."

"You don't need to stay back with me, Farhan. I'm sure it's bound to be unpleasant once they know about our divorce. I'll probably stay there for a week at the most, maybe even less."

"Only if you're sure."

"I am."

"Okay then. I'll book our tickets and call you back," said Farhan before disconnecting the call.

The next day, Anya had opted to have lunch with Shaan and the others at the community kitchen as Dev had gone to Mumbai with Meena for a routine health check up for her. Feeling too full, she decided to take a stroll along the lake. "Shaan, I'll be back in half an hour, just going for a walk," she called out, stepping out of the office when he nodded.

The sunlight was a pleasure to walk in, in the February cold, even though it was midday. Anya strolled along the perimeter, hugging her body as a cool breeze blew from the lake. She removed the sweater which she had knotted around her neck and pulled it on, leaving the buttons open. Walking further down, she stood next to the short wall lining the lake for a few metres. While most of the lake surrounding was open, Dev had had a wall built in this section as it was the deepest here. There was even a marker which said that it was fifteen to twenty feet deep in that area. It was probably closer to twenty now since the monsoons had got over only a few months ago.

Anya absent-mindedly threw small pebbles into the water, watching the ripples. While she appreciated the alone time, she missed Dev. As she stood there day-dreaming, she heard footsteps and turned her head to see who it was. "Hello Renu," said Anya, her smile not reaching her eyes, wondering what the other woman was doing here. It was obvious that Renu did not like her, though Anya could not really understand why.

"Hello bitch," said Renu, glaring at Anya's shocked face. "Why are you shocked? It's because of you that my life has gone down the drain. Before you came, Dev was happy with me. But now that you are here, he refuses to even look at me," she snarled.

Anya was unwilling to believe that. She would have known. Dev's body language around Renu always suggested abject dislike. It was obvious that he put up with his neighbour only because of good manners.

"You don't believe me," said Renu, her voice going calm. "It doesn't matter now, anyway."

Before Anya could understand what she meant, Renu rushed towards her, giving her a hard push over the wall which was barely three feet high. Not expecting the attack, Anya's eyes widened in shock as she went over swiftly, her arms flailing, a scream on her lips before she heard a splash and then absolute silence as she went under.

Renu dusted her hands and walked towards her jeep, getting into it, and driving away as if the devil was on her tail.

Shaan looked at the wall clock in the office. It was forty minutes since Anya was gone. One thing he had come to know about Anya was that she was never late and she was not one to shirk work. Dev had told him specifically to look out for her as she was still recovering her strength. Shaan got up, feeling restless, his instincts shouting out that something was amiss. He speed-dialled Anya's cell, only for it to ring from where it was lying next to her laptop on the main desk.

He stepped out of the office and got on his bicycle, wondering which way Anya must have gone. That was when he noticed Renu racing away in her jeep. He frowned. What was she doing on Wadhwa Farm, when Dev was not home? He pedalled faster, going towards the lake in the direction from which Renu's jeep had come.

As he reached the wall, he was surprised to see a totally wet Anya, trying to grab a hold as she attempted to get out of the water. Her face pale, she gave him a weak grin, her teeth chattering. "Give me a hand, Shaan," she called out as he jogged closer to her. "Am I glad to see you!"

Shaan took out his cell phone and dialled with his left hand, even as he pulled Anya out of the water with his right. "Dharmesh Uncle, can you please get the car to the lake near the wall? It's urgent," he said.

Anya sat on the wall; her clothes sodden as she tried to squeeze the excess water out. Shaan helped her out of her wet shoes, removing his jacket to cover her shoulders from the biting cold breeze.

"Is something wrong Shaan?" asked Dharmesh, "Dev just arrived with *Daadima*. I..."

Dev had taken the phone from Dharmesh by now and asked, "What happened, Shaan? What's the emergency?"

"Anya fell into the lake. She's out now, but..."

"We are on our way," said Dev and the phone went silent.

They arrived almost immediately, the station wagon screeching to a stop a few feet from where Shaan's cycle lay on the ground. Dev jumped out of the car and went to Anya. "What happened, sweetheart?" he asked, lifting her up in his arms to take her to the car. "Shaan, will you call Dr. Sriram?"

"I don't think I really need a doctor," protested Anya, her voice stronger than before. "Dev, careful where you put me in the car, I'm totally wet."

Dev placed her gently next to *Daadima*, taking a blanket from the back and wrapping it around her. When Dharmesh started the car, Dev called Seema to ask her to run a hot bath for Anya.

"So how did your visit to the doctor go, *Daadima*?" asked Anya to the silent Meena.

Meena smiled at the bedraggled girl sitting beside her. "All good. I'm as fit as a horse. But how did you fall into the lake Anya? Did you think that the afternoon is a good time to swim in this chilly weather?" she teased her gently.

Anya gave *Daadima* a smile, snuggling against Dev's chest as he held her close to his warm body. "You know something *Daadima*, today I found out that I can swim, almost champion level."

"Are you saying you deliberately jumped into the lake Anya?" Dev's grey eyes turned tempestuous as he looked into her eyes. "Are you crazy or what? You didn't know that you could swim. What if something had happened to you?" He shut his eyes, thoroughly shaken at the picture of Anya's lifeless body floating on the surface of the lake sprang before his mind's eye.

Opening his eyes, Dev shook her hard, forgetting to be gentle for the first time. "How dare you? Couldn't you have waited for me?" His eyes blazed with temper. He had not noticed that the car had come to a stop outside their home.

Shaan had followed them on his bike, holding on to the car's fender. Bending down to open the car door when it stopped at the farmhouse, he heard Dev and said quietly, his voice serious. "I don't think Anya chose to swim in the lake." He was still shaken by the incident, more than Anya it seemed.

"What?" Dev's head jerked to Shaan and then back to Anya, even as he pulled her out of the car, his hold rough. "Just a minute *Daadima*, let me open the door for you."

"You get Anya to her room Dev. Dharmesh is here to help me. Go on," said Meena.

Dev nodded before looking down at Anya as she stood beside him, his eyes still smouldering with anger. "What Shaan is saying; is that right?" asked Dev.

"Yes, he's right. Renu pushed me into the lake." When she heard Dev curse, Anya pouted at him saying, "But Dev, one good thing came out of that. I know now that I am a strong swimmer." She had never seen him lose his cool before now.

Dev gave her an intense stare. "Not funny, Anya. Shaan, can you organise some hot, sweet tea with a shot of brandy? Make that three cups. I think you and I can do with one too," he smiled at his manager, patting him on his shoulder.

Dev lifted Anya in his arms, ignoring her protests. "I'm okay Dev. I can walk. I'm way stronger than before," she smiled, patting his manly cheek, his temper exciting her more than anything.

While he noticed the shimmering excitement in her eyes, Dev refused to give in to temptation. He shuddered when he thought again of what could have happened *if* Anya had not known how to swim and he wanted to throttle Renu with his bare hands.

Seema was just stepping out of Anya's bedroom, her bath almost ready. "Come Anya, let me help you get out of your wet clothes," offered Seema.

Anya raised an eyebrow at Dev, challenge in her brown eyes, before saying with a smile, "I can manage Seema Aunty. I don't feel all that weak."

"It would be great if you can get some tea ready, Seema Aunty," requested Dev, "I'm not really sure Shaan knows how to make tea."

Once she left, Dev shut Anya's bedroom door, pulling her into his arms, even as he removed her clothes in a hurry. He got her naked in record time, before carrying her into the bathroom. "Do you want to join me?" asked Anya, her voice hoarse with want as she sank luxuriously into the hot tub.

He shook his head, regret in his eyes. "Later tonight. I have a Jacuzzi in my bathroom," he promised. "I'd better go. Will you be able to manage? Or shall I send Seema Aunty up again?"

"You mean you aren't going to wash my back?" she pouted at him cutely.

Dev went on his knees beside the tub, giving her a hard kiss. "I need to do something urgently. I'll be back soon." He turned around and left, not saying anything further.

Dev did not stop to have his brandy laced tea, getting into the station wagon to drive to his neighbour's home. He was glad that Renu was nowhere around or he might have just throttled her. Seeing her father in the big hall of their house, Dev greeted, "Hello Uncle."

"Dev *beta*, welcome, welcome. This is a pleasant surprise. Sit down. Aunty is getting tea. You must also have a cup."

Dev refused the tea and spoke to Renu's father for the next fifteen minutes, without interruption.

After hearing him out, Mr. Gurnani said, "Oh, but Renu has set her heart on marrying you." He was terribly disappointed, shaking his head. His daughter was headstrong and he had so hoped a tough man like Dev would be perfect for keeping her in line.

"I'm sorry to disappoint you, Uncle, but that thought has never crossed my mind. You heard my offer. Tell me when you are ready." Dev left, wishing the older man a good evening.

He stepped out of the house to see Renu getting out of her jeep. "Devvvv... how wonderful to see you," she gushed, walking close to him.

"Don't you dare lay a finger on me, unless you want a hard slap," snarled Dev.

"Oh! So Anya's alive," said Renu, a sneer on her face which had suddenly turned ugly.

"No thanks to you," said Dev, getting into his station wagon and roaring away.

Renu's parents discussed through the evening and decided to take Dev's offer of buying their land along with the house. They were too old to run the farm and their only child was so not interested. They refused to listen to their daughter's protests, for once putting their foot down.

"I don't want to leave the farm," argued Renu, stamping her foot in a rage.

"Listen Renu," said her father, "This is the only way. Dev promised not to go to the police on the condition that we shift from here. It's a good thing that he's ready to buy our farm at the prevailing market price."

"Who is he to lay down conditions?" snarled Renu.

"That's all because of you," said her mother, gritting her teeth, "You and your temper. It's my fault that you have become the spoilt brat that you are."

For the first time in twenty-eight years, Renu's tantrums got her nowhere. Her parents were keen to hold on to the little bit of respect they still held in the society. They thanked their stars for Dev's levelheadedness in sorting the issue amicably without bringing the law on their heads.

nya flew to Chandigarh with Farhan two days later, refusing to give in to the feeling of nervousness. "They know we are visiting them today, right?" she asked for the third time.

"Yes, sweetie," he said, holding her cold hand tightly in his. It was four in the evening when they knocked on the door of Anya's home. She, of course, did not recognise the medium-sized bungalow. Amal opened the door the moment they rang the bell. "Anya, *meri bacchi*," she cried out, holding her hands out to her.

Anya placed her hands in the older woman's hesitantly, her eyes searching Amal's face.

"Come in; Farhan, you too. What? You both have only one small bag? Don't tell me you are going to stay for only a short time." Amal chattered as she pulled Anya inside their home. "Pappa's gone to get your favourite *gulab jamoon*. I'd have made some at home, but I haven't been keeping well lately."

"What's wrong, Aunty?" asked Farhan solicitously.

Anya did not open her mouth, taking in her surroundings. The living room was big and airy, with four doors opening from it.

"Come and sit down, *beta*. What are you looking at? As if you have not seen the house before," said Amal, biting sarcasm in her voice.

Anya turned to stare at the woman who called herself her mother, a small frown puckering her forehead. "Well, I don't remember this house. That's why I was looking. I hope you don't mind."

"What?!" screeched Amal. "Are you saying that you still can't remember anything? Farhan, I told you that doctor was useless. Now see what has happened. Anya still can't remember anything." She turned to her daughter and asked, "But you know that I'm your mother, *na*?"

Anya's voice came in a whisper as she shook her head. "No, I don't." She probably would have felt a connection if the older woman had given her a hug. But nothing! There was no affection at all there.

"What is this, Farhan?" growled Amal angrily.

He shrugged. "That's how it is, Aunty. When do you think Uncle will get back home?" He had already booked his return flight for later in the night.

Gaurav entered the house even as he asked. "Anya, Farhan, welcome home. I'm…"

Amal shrieked, without letting her husband talk further. "*Kyunji*, Anya still can't remember her past," she howled.

"Is that so?" asked Gaurav, looking at his daughter who was still standing in the middle of the room. He went up to her and gave her an awkward hug, as if he had never done it before today. He gave a sigh saying, "Why don't we all sit down? Amal, can we have some tea?" After learning about Anya's illness, Gaurav had studied a bit about the subject of amnesia at the local library and better understood the situation. While he had tried explaining it to his wife a couple of times, he had given up once he realised that she was not interested.

"Tea? Are you crazy?" screamed Amal at her husband. "My own daughter refuses to recognise me and you want to have tea?"

"Yes, that's right," said her husband firmly. "For the last time, it's not as if Anya doesn't want to recognise us. She can't."

Farhan looked at the older man with respect. Finally! Finally Gaurav Chhabria was talking sense.

Amal turned towards the kitchen in a huff, unable to refuse her husband's bidding. She brought out the tea which she had already made and sat down on the sofa next to her husband.

"Okay, Uncle, Aunty. It's like this." Farhan did not want to beat around the bush. "Anya and I are divorced. We..." He stopped talking when he heard a keening noise. It was Anya's mother, howling her heart out.

Amal beat herself on her chest, cursing him. "How dare you ditch her when she needs you?" she shouted at him.

Anya raised a hand to stop both the crying and the abuse. "Aunty, I..."

"Aunty?! I'm your mother," protested Amal shrilly.

Anya cleared her throat which felt choked, taking a sip of tea before speaking again. "Okay, Mom. I..."

"Call me Mamma. That's what you've always called me," cried out Amal.

Anya shut her eyes for a few seconds, trying to gather her wits about her. All the screeching and screaming had shot her nerves. For a minute, she wondered if she should leave along with Farhan. But no, Anya straightened her shoulders. She was no coward. Drinking her tea in gulps, she placed the cup down and spoke again. "Mamma, Pappa, listen. Farhan and I got divorced even before my accident. I had told him not to inform you people. He is not responsible for my accident, nor has he ditched me. And come on, I'm an adult. I don't need someone to care for me twenty-four-seven. I can manage to survive." She looked at her father appealingly. He had given her a hug, after all. Maybe she shared a better relationship with him.

Gaurav stared at his daughter and then at the man who he had believed was his son-in-law. What was with this modern generation? How could they treat marriage so lightly? He shook his head, opening and shutting his mouth, too stunned to say anything. "Farhan?" he appealed to the younger man. "Why?"

"I'm gay, Uncle. I never wanted to get married. I…"

"Then why the hell did you marry my daughter?" snarled Gaurav. When he heard his wife shriek once again, he turned to see that she had laid her head on the back of the sofa, her face white with shock.

"Anya didn't want to get married either. But you and Aunty gave her no choice. So…"

"Anya?" asked Gaurav. "What do you have to say about this?"

She shrugged; her face expressionless. "Nothing. I can't recall a damn thing."

"And so you two decided to get married, making fools of us," said Gaurav, too angry by now. "Well, Uncle. It wasn't as if we wanted to make fools of you both. It's just that we wanted to be left alone to lead our lives peacefully. We stayed together, married in name only, for two years. And then we got divorced, on the same day that Anya had the accident. No," Farhan raised a hand to stop Gaurav from interrupting him, "I wasn't with her. We had gone our separate ways by then. And we weren't planning to tell you unless it was absolutely necessary. You need to understand something Uncle. It's only in India that parents have such a stranglehold on their children's lives. Come on, we are adults, almost twenty-five. Why can't we lead independent lives?" Farhan's voice was bitter now, as he could not help thinking of his own parents who had disowned him.

Gaurav opened and shut his mouth several times now. He really did not know what to say. The situation was too bizarre for words. After a few minutes of silence—yes, even Amal had been rendered speechless for the first time in her life—he asked, "So what happens now?"

Farhan was glad to hear those words, giving a sigh of relief. "Anya will be here for a few days. She's your daughter, so I'm sure you don't mind. And…"

"What about our relatives, neighbours, and friends? What do we tell them?" Amal was sitting straighter now, battle in her stance, as she glared at Farhan.

"Why Aunty? Nothing. You don't owe an explanation to anyone. Anya's your child and she has come visiting. How is it anyone else's business?" asked Farhan logically.

"What if they ask why she's divorced?" Amal began to cry again.

"Mamma," said Anya, trying her best to keep her voice soothing, "Why tell anyone I'm divorced at all?"

Gaurav nodded his head vigorously. "Anya's right," he told his wife. "Why tell anyone about it? And what happens after you leave here? Where will you live? What will you do?" He did not want to be bothered. But his conscience troubled him.

"Just as Farhan said, I'm an adult, Pappa. I have a well-paying job, with accommodation. I'll be fine." She did not want to get into too many details as that probably would have given birth to more questions.

Gaurav sighed heavily, shaking his head. It was a rare occasion when he did not feel in control. But right now, it looked like there was nothing he could do to change his daughter's life. She was here for but a few days. He decided to make her stay as pleasant as possible.

"So, Uncle, Aunty," said Farhan, getting up. "I'll take your leave."

Amal looked at him, tears rolling down her face. "I feel so sad, *beta*."

Farhan hugged her. "Don't worry Aunty. Everything will turn out for the best." He shook Gaurav's hand before turning to Anya. He opened his arms wide to pull her close. "You take care, Anya. I can't face Dev if something happens to you," he whispered for her ears alone.

Anya gave him a weak grin, a sigh whooshing from her unexpectedly. "I should be alright," she said, walking with him to the door.

Gaurav and Anya chatted about politics and sports, refusing to touch on anything personal, while Amal got dinner ready. They could hear her loud sniffs from where they sat the living room, but refused to acknowledge them.

Dinner was a quiet affair, Amal giving her daughter irritated glances while the latter pecked at her food, her appetite non-existent. Immediately after it was over, Anya got up. "Can you please tell me where my room is? I'm too tired and would like to go to sleep," she said.

"What? You don't even know where your room is?" Amal asked her.

Gaurav laid a pacifying hand on his wife's arm. "Of course, she doesn't. Let me show her." He guided Anya up the stairs to the first floor, opening the first door on the right. "This is your room, *beta*. It's exactly how it was when you left."

"Thank you, Pappa." Anya hugged him, feeling bad for him suddenly. "I'm very tired Pappa. We'll talk in the morning, okay?"

Gaurav nodded, leaving her at her door.

Anya stood at the entrance to her room, staring, looking for a clue, anything which would tell her that she had lived in this room before. After fifteen minutes, she gave up, changing into her nightclothes and crashing on the bed. She sent Dev a message, promising to call him the next day. She knew that he must be worried. But then, so was she. Dev would understand, she knew.

She went to sleep with a smile on her lips, forgetting her parents as she thought of Dev.

Dev was feeling rather lost, sitting at the breakfast table next to his grandmother, staring into space. He turned when he felt a touch on his shoulder.

"What happened Dev? Are you missing Anya too much? She'll be back in a week. I wouldn't worry if I were you," said Meena reassuringly.

Dev sighed. "I suppose, *Daadima*. I'm sorry that I'm such poor company."

"Don't be silly. You know that I don't mind that. Tell me, did you talk to Renu?" she asked.

"Oh, I forgot to mention. I spoke to her dad. He's selling the farm to us and moving to Pune. The registration papers are being drawn as we talk."

"However did you manage that?" asked Meena, admiration in her voice. She was proud of her grandson.

Dev grinned at her. "I told him that I won't go to the police if they agreed to move. It was his idea to sell the farm to me. By the way, Renu's dad had been under the impression that I wanted to marry her." He grimaced. "Don't know how the hell he had arrived at that conclusion."

Meena smiled wisely. "Renu has wanted to marry you for years."

"What?! You knew about it *Daadima*? I wish you'd told me. I'd have nipped the thought in the bud."

Meena nodded sagely. "I suppose. For such a shrewd businessman and a successful farmer, you don't really know how a devious female's mind works, do you?" She gave him an affectionate smile.

"That must be because I live with a grand old woman who is all heart," he said, giving his grandmother a hug.

Three days had gone by and Anya had got into a routine at her parents' home. She spoke to Dev everyday and that was probably the one thing which kept her grounded. Amal continued to sniffle whenever she set her eyes on her daughter. But Anya decided to ignore that, helping her mother in her daily chores as much as she could.

"Anya has changed," whispered Amal to her husband. "She never used to help me at home, before."

"But Anya was studying in those days. She had too many things to do, like projects and all. She never had the time to help you. It's different now, isn't it?" said Gaurav logically.

"I knew it. You will *never* agree with me, whatever I say." Amal jumped up from the sofa where she had been sitting next to her husband, walking away in a huff, her husband's soft laughter following her.

Anya had climbed up on a tall stool in the kitchen, cleaning the shelves which were out of reach. She removed an old cooking pot which had obviously not been used for a long time. "Mamma," she called out, "Didn't you used to make Sindhi *kadi* in this? Don't you use it anymore?"

Amal had walked into the kitchen on hearing Anya's voice. "Oh that! No *beta*. Those days we were in a joint family. The pot was required as I used to cook in large quantities. But now, with only the two of us, we… wait a minute! How do you know about the pot?" she frowned up at her daughter, "I thought you couldn't remember anything." Her voice had gone up by several decibels.

A startled Anya dropped the metal pot and the sound rang like a gunshot, bringing Gaurav rushing into the kitchen. Anya swayed on top of the stool, holding her head as if in pain. "Pappa, Mamma. I…"

She would have fallen if Gaurav had not given her a hand, helping her down from the stool. He placed an arm around her shoulders, guiding her slowly to the hall and making her sit on the sofa. "Amal, get her some water to drink," he called out to his hovering wife.

Anya had turned pale as memories gushed into her mind. The clouds which had submerged everything, suddenly drifted away as everything came back to her, in colourful pictures, with dialogues.

"Anya, don't go out wearing such a short dress. People will stare at you." That was her mother calling out to her when she was barely twelve years old.

"Don't talk to the boys, okay? Badima warned me that you always speak only to the boys. Next time I hear a complaint, I'll wring your ears." The fourteen-year-old

Anya gave her mother a rebellious stare and poked her tongue out when Amal turned her back.

"I don't know what you will do, but you have to come first in your class. Look at your cousin Shibu, he's always at the top of his class." The constant comparison irritated the hell out of the fifteen-year-old Anya. While she had gone on to complete her MBA with flying colours, Shibu had got married to the woman he had raped. But then, he was a man. He could even get away with murder in the Chhabria family.

Gaurav spoke to Anya on the phone when she was staying with her uncle's family, the Madhvanis, in Mumbai. Just turned nineteen, Anya was taking a break after giving her entrance exam for MBA. "Beta, an excellent alliance has come for you. Fix kardhoon? That boy's name is Dev Wadhwa. He's an MBA from America. His parents are keen to have you for their daughter-in-law."

Anya frowned. She had spent time with Dev only the previous evening, in secret. It had been such fun and she had liked him, a lot. But marriage? No way. There was too much to do in life and she was too young to tie the knot with a stranger. She made it clear to her father that she wanted to study further. "I'm too young Pappa. Maybe after I finish my post graduation. Not now, please."

Amal had called her a day later to say, "We have booked your return ticket. Come back home immediately."

"What? Why Mamma? I'm having so much fun here."

"Your uncle doesn't want you to stay there, not after refusing the alliance. The Wadhwas are their neighbours and they are ashamed to face them. Luckily for us, the boy is a farmer. Which girl wants to marry a farmer and live a hard life?" Amal said smugly. "You just come back home."

Anya went stiff, opening her eyes suddenly, saying, "Dev."

Oh my God! Dev and she had known each other from before. She went hot and then she went cold as she stared into nothing. Anya got up suddenly to pace the floor, marching up and down, her hands locked behind her back. She recalled their tryst to the coffee shop at Kharghar, the long motorbike ride which had led up to it.

And… and, Anya felt her heartbeat pick up speed when she remembered her last meeting with Dev, five years ago.

The younger Anya had been totally floored by the handsome Dev, especially his excellent manners, after the time they had spent at the coffee shop. It was past eleven in the night when she had gone up to the terrace the next night, once the rest of the family had settled down, hoping against hope that Dev would also turn up there. She had not been disappointed when she saw him sitting on his terrace, across the wall. He had turned his phone off the moment he noticed her and jumped over to her side with a smile on his face.

"Hey, I was hoping you'd turn up."

Anya pressed a hand to her stomach, trying to still the butterflies which seemed to be kicking up a storm within. She felt choked when she looked up at Dev's classic features, excitement pounding within her. She pressed the other hand against the first one so that it would not be obvious to him that she was trembling. Only she was not aware how her glowing brown eyes gave her feelings away to the man standing too close to her. Doing her best to tone down her gasping breaths, Anya whispered with a challenging tilt of her head, "Were you?"

Dev grinned at her. "You mean you weren't expecting me?"

She shook her head, biting her lips alternatively, to stop the answering smile which was waiting to burst forth. "No."

"I'll go then," said Dev, turning around, without taking a single step forward.

"Please don't," said the young Anya, stopping him with a hand on his arm.

He caught the trembling hand and turned back to her, the smile disappearing from his grey eyes when he saw the expression on her face. "Anya..." His touch as light as a feather, Dev traced the side of her face, appearing fascinated with the curl of dark, silky hair which clung to his forefinger.

She stared up into his eyes, her lips parted, her white teeth gleaming in the soft moonlight. Would he kiss her? Maybe he would not. Anya eyed his masculine lips, the upper one thin and the lower one broad and sensual. What would it feel like?

Dev took her small chin between his thumb and forefinger, bringing her face closer to his. "Anya... you don't know how tempting you are. I..."

Not really aware of what she was doing, Anya went on her toes, placing her hands on his shoulders for support before pressing her lips to his. A sigh shuddered through her being when she felt his hard arms going around her as he gathered her close. Her breathing stopped when she felt his damp tongue trace the shape of her lips. Sensations flooded her body as if all of her nerves ended right there at her lips. She was lost for she knew not how long before Dev shifted away with a jerk, moving her body away from his.

"My God! Anya..." he shook his head.

She could see the colour running up his cheeks. Was he embarrassed? Why had he stopped? Did he not like the kiss? For Anya, the kiss had literally rocked her world. Would he kiss her again?

"Good night, Anya." Dev walked away from her, jumping over the wall, and rushing towards the staircase with a small wave.

Anya had felt absolutely dejected; her young heart crushed. Dev had not wanted to kiss her again.

That was the last time she had met him in private before her father had called her back home.

Dev was the reason why she had never found a boyfriend. He was also the reason why she had not wanted to get married when her parents wanted her to. He was her first crush and he had spoilt her for all other men. Thanks to Farhan she had escaped being tied to someone she did not love.

Anya shook her head, amazed at how destiny had brought Dev and her together. If that was the case, then she must thank her lucky stars she had met with the accident that Friday morning. Coming to a decision, she turned to her parents. Anya took a deep breath before she started to speak to them. No, the days of hiding things from her parents were gone. It was time to be truthful. If they accepted her, well and good; if they did not, well, there was not much she could do about it.

"Mamma, Pappa. I remember everything now," said Anya, a serene smile on her face. She told them everything—why she and Farhan had got married, why they had got divorced, how Dev had cared for her after the accident. "Dev Wadhwa, the farmer, the alliance we refused—he's the same guy you met at the hospital, holding my hand. There are farmers and there are farmers, Pappa. Dev has twenty-five, no, thirty acres of land and he simply mints money. He lives with his grandmother in a sprawling bungalow. He has forty-plus people working for him. Even I work for him as his marketing manager." She paused for breath, happy that the two of them were listening to her without interrupting. "Dev and I are in love with each other. He wants to marry me and I would be honoured to be his wife. But I wanted to visit here just in case I could recall my previous life. And I did that only because Dev suggested it." She gave them a wide smile. "And it worked. And you know what? I'm so glad I got to spend time with you both, Mamma and Pappa."

She got up again. "I want to go back to Karjat today. What I would like is for the two of you to visit Wadhwa Farm and stay back for our wedding and give us your blessings." She went on her knees in front of her stunned parents. "Please, will you do that for me?"

Gaurav held his wife's hand when she would have protested, shaking his head at her. "Yes, Anya *beta*. We'll do that. Do you have to get back today itself?"

"Yes Pappa. Dev has been too worried about me. I want to get back soon and give him a surprise."

"I understand," said Gaurav. "You have our blessings."

"Thank you, Pappa." Anya got up to kiss her father on his cheek, before turning to her mother, bending down to give her a kiss too. Amal touched her cheek in wonder, having never been an affectionate person. "Okay guys, I need to rush. Let me pack and get myself to the airport."

She got out of the Mumbai airport at five in the evening, hiring a taxi to Karjat. Jumping into the cab, Anya gave the driver the directions before calling Farhan. "Hey, guess what?" she said with a smile in her voice.

"You remember," he declared.

"Yes!"

"Where are you?"

"I just got into a taxi outside Mumbai airport. I'm on my way to Dev's farm. He's in for a surprise."

"You mean he doesn't know yet?"

"Nope," said Anya, grinning from ear to ear. She chatted with Farhan for some time before disconnecting. She willed the car to eat the miles faster than ever as she could not wait to see Dev again. It was a good thing that they always talked in the mornings. He would not try to reach her now, or her surprise would turn anti-climax.

It was eight when Anya's taxi entered the farm gates. The driver jumped out to open them, driving inside. "You can shut them on your way back," she instructed him, excitement making her pulse flare up. She could see the bright lights of the farmhouse even from this far. It took them all of five minutes to reach the portico.

Surprised to hear a vehicle at that hour, Dev got up and went to the door. He was amazed and thrilled to see Anya getting out of the taxi. "Hey," he called out, a wide smile of welcome on his face.

Anya turned to him, glad when the taxi took an about turn and moved towards the gate. "Dev." She rushed into his wide-open arms, clinging to him, pulling his head down for a much-needed kiss. She smiled suddenly when Dev lifted his head as they came up for air. She had not imagined it when she had found Dev's kiss familiar when they first made love at her apartment.

"This is such a wonderful surprise, sweetheart. How come you decided to return so suddenly?" With their arms around each other, they stepped into the doorway.

"I remember, Dev," she said. Her voice, though quiet, was feverish with excitement.

"What?! How?!" He stopped midstride, turning to her.

"Oh Dev! Isn't it a miracle that we've met again, after all these years?" She hugged him tightly, burying her face on his chest. "I never forgot you, especially your kiss." She lifted her head to look up at him, her chocolate eyes shining with love. "You know something? You were—are—my first crush, and the last. I never could stomach the idea of marrying any other man. And Dev," she pulled his head down to whisper in his ear, "I'm so glad you never married."

Dev crushed her closer to his body, pressing his lips to her forehead. "Every woman who came into my life fell short of my expectations as I kept comparing her with you, my darling Anya. You had totally bewitched me."

"But Dev," Anya's eyes darkened with remembered hurt, "You went away after kissing me. What did I do wrong?"

"Wrong?" Dev lifted his head to look down at the love of his life, a small frown on his face. "I don't understand. That was the most perfect kiss I have ever shared with anyone in my life."

"Then why did you walk away immediately after? I thought you didn't like kissing me." Anya's voice trembled with the memory of her hurt.

"Oh Anya!" Dev pressed his forehead against hers. "I'm terribly sorry if that's the impression I gave you. My sweetheart," he whispered into her ear, tracing the shell-like shape with his tongue, "Your kiss plucked at my heartstrings, too hard. Will you believe me if I say that I ran away scared of the emotions you invoked in me?"

Anya's eyes went wide as she looked at Dev. He had appeared so confident, even that many years ago, that she could not imagine him being scared of anything. But again, she could relate to what he was saying. While the kiss they shared had been absolutely exciting, Anya had not been ready for any kind of commitment at that time either. She grinned at him teasingly. "Dev Wadhwa ran away scared. Are you sure you want to marry me now?"

"Never more so," he growled, nipping at her ear lobe. "If I remember right, you still haven't accepted my proposal of marriage."

"Ask me again," she commanded, confidence brimming in her eyes as she looked up at the man she had fallen in love with.

Dev lifted her high up in his arms, shaking his head at her, a wide smile on his lips. "No more asking. We'll be married in three weeks."

"Masterful, are we?" Anya giggled, bending down to claim his lips in a sizzling kiss.

EPILOGUE

ev and Anya were married at the farm three weeks later with *Daadima's* blessings as she sat next to the bride and groom, grinning from ear to ear, in the open courtyard, with the sun shining down on them. While both sets of parents, Farhan, Arth and some close friends attended the wedding, the bride and groom were happiest with the presence of all the farm workers, their four dogs and five cats.

The wedding feast was lavish. Seema and her team were given an off so that they could enjoy the wedding ceremony and an outsider had been given the contract. Everyone enjoyed themselves immensely, blessing the couple with a long, married life.

While Dev was not anywhere near to forgiving his parents, Anya had worked hard at bridging the gap. Yes, it would take time and they might never get all that close, but they were at least on speaking terms.

While Karishma and Durgesh Wadhwa still could not see the wisdom in farming, they were absolutely impressed that their son had become a billionaire and even graced the pages of newspapers and magazines. The grown-up Jai and Chaahat knew for a fact that their older brother was a supreme success. They even planned to wangle a holiday job with him come summer.

Gaurav was extremely happy that his daughter had finally settled down. More than anything, the boy seemed very decent and was obviously rich. He had strictly warned Amal against throwing tantrums. But she still managed to say in a loud whisper, "Is Anya stupid or what? How can she invite her ex-husband to her wedding? What will Dev think of her?"

While Gaurav was also worried about the fact, he decided not to say anything. Farhan had been right. They were all adults and should be allowed to live their lives the way they chose to.

After the wedding lunch, Shaan transported the married couple by helicopter to Ravine Hotel in Panchgani. He gave them a drop and left almost immediately to return home.

Dev had booked a valley facing room in the hotel for three days. While they planned to go on a proper honeymoon to Europe in April, they did not step out of the room on all three days, ordering all their meals there.

Dev and Anya were sharing a bottle of chilled sparkling wine, in bed, as they gazed at the luscious green valley below. Anya sat between Dev's widespread legs as he leaned against the headboard. He nibbled on her neck and shoulder between sips of wine. Anya returned the compliment by munching on his fingers. Placing his hand against her breast, she stretched luxuriously, pressing her back to his hard chest. Turning on her side, she whispered into his ear, "Aren't I the lucky one?!" Anya paused as she took a deep breath, inhaling Dev's masculine scent which was so uniquely his. "I love you Dev," she told him, her cocoa eyes twinkling with happiness.

"That you are. I love you too, babe," he said, laughter in his grey eyes.

She punched him on his shoulder, giving him a mock glare. "You meanie! You missed your cue to say how lucky you are."

He shrugged, giving her a hard kiss. "But of course, I am." He reached a hand to caress her bottom. "It's just that you look gorgeous when you get into battle mode." He bent down to take an engorged nipple into his mouth, suckling her softly at first and then hard.

"Dev..." she moaned. "I want you inside me, now."

He pushed her back on the bed to climb on top of her. "I can't have enough of you, sweetheart." He took her hand and placed it against his throbbing shaft.

She rubbed a delighted hand over him, saying, "You are always ready!"

"You bet I am."

They made long and leisurely love, riding the waves together to reach an incredible climax. Anya lay in Dev's arms, spooned against his body, his leg straddling over both of hers.

"I'm still finding it amazing, how we met each other after all these years," said Anya, wonder in her voice.

"Tell me about it," he said, nuzzling the back of her neck. "That day when the accident happened, I was shocked beyond words when I saw you lying there, pale and still. I think I stopped breathing for a minute before I discovered that your pulse was beating." He shuddered, recalling the incident. He had never spoken about it to her.

"Did you never want to get married Dev?" she asked, turning her head on the pillow to look at him.

"Every time I thought of settling down with a wife and family, it was your face which came in front of me. With so much to do, I didn't bother to do anything about it."

"It was meant to be, wasn't it?" she smiled.

"Finding my Anya, yes!"

THE END

OTHER BOOKS
BY
SUNDARI
VENKATRAMAN

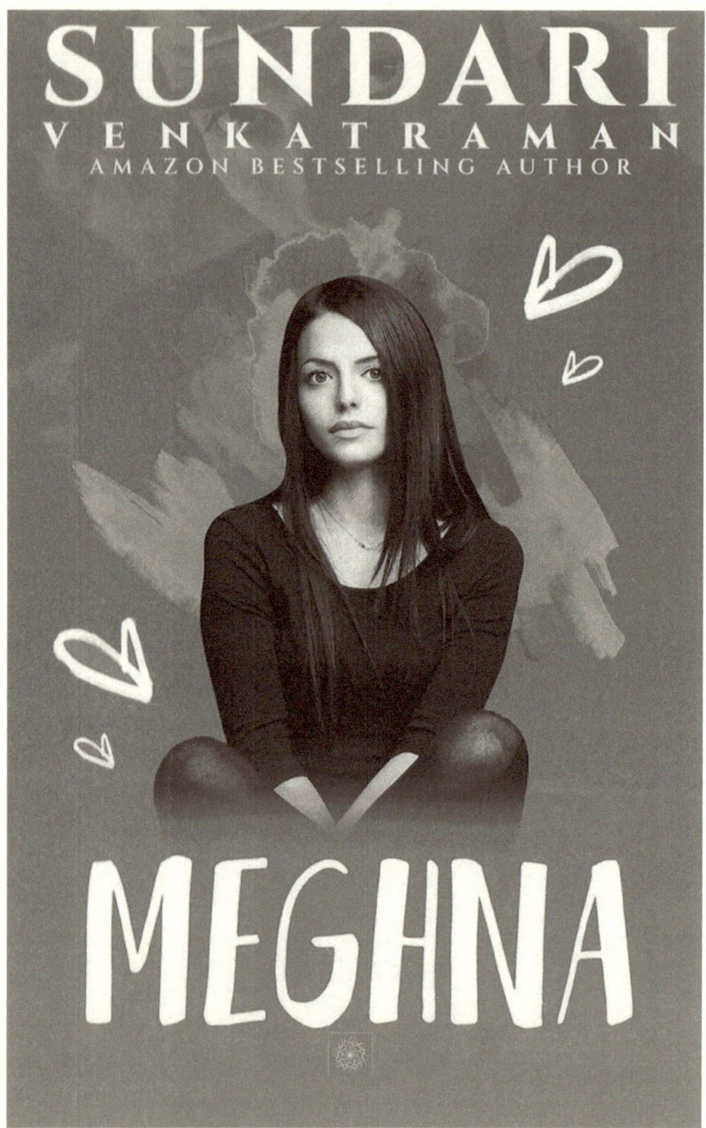

SUNDARI
VENKATRAMAN
AMAZON BESTSELLING AUTHOR
MEGHNA

The young and dashing Rahul Sinha lives in England with his parents, Shyam and Rajni. He is an only son of the rich banker. Rahul is totally attached to his father but does not care for his mother. Read the book to find out why....

Rahul is exulted with his efforts at work paying off and plans a holiday with his best friend Sanjay Srivastav who lives in Mumbai with his wife Reema, kids Sasha and Rehaan and most importantly, his sister, Meghna. Rahul recalls meeting Meghna just before they parted six years ago.

Meghna works for a website and also teaches modern dance as she loves it. She's thrown for a toss when Rahul comes visiting. She had thought he had forgotten them.

But how could Rahul do that? Sanjay's his best friend and Rahul had always treated their home as his own. Sanjay's mother had been more of a mother to Rahul than his own. Rahul had stayed away after moving to England or so Meghna believes.

Thus begins the story of Rahul and Meghna, the teasing, the flirting, the anger, the tears...

...will they find love?

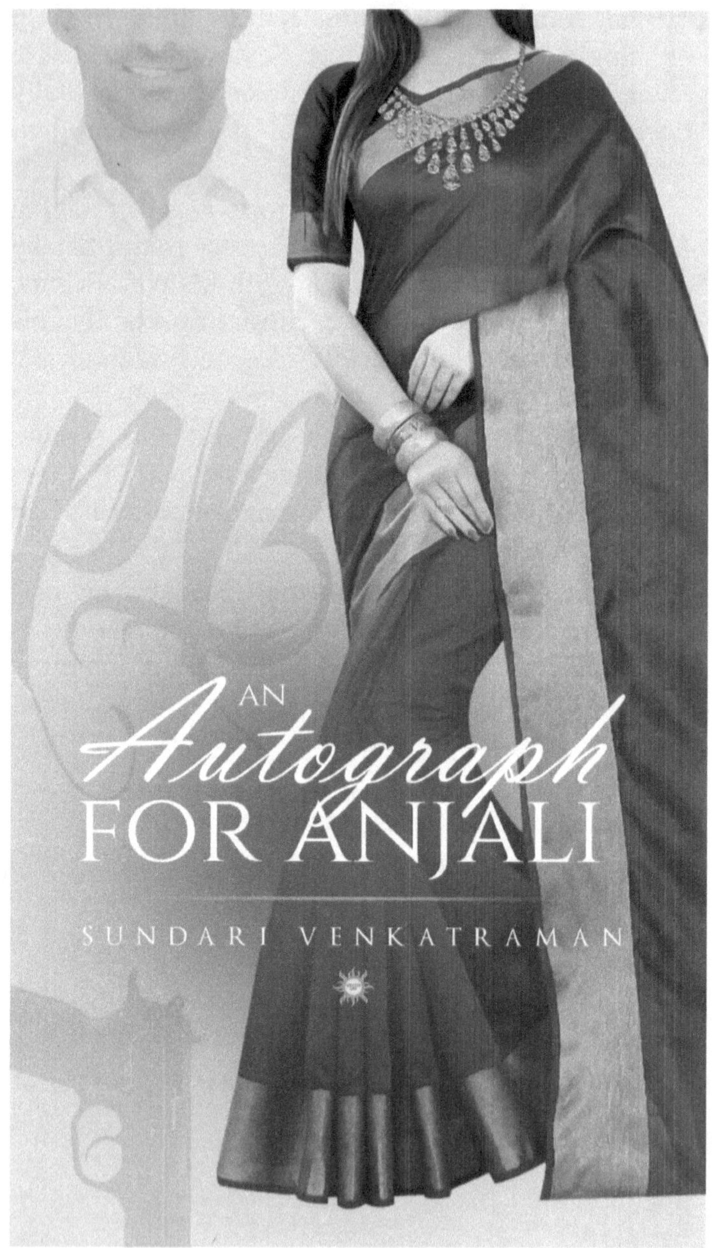

AN
Autograph
FOR ANJALI
SUNDARI VENKATRAMAN

At thirty-nine, Anjali Mathur feels like an exotic bird trapped in a golden cage, hating the life of the idle wife of a multi-millionaire husband who simply has neither the time nor the inclination to give her his attention.

She meets Parth at a common friend's party. It's not just his looks that Anjali's attracted to, but his gentle and understanding nature.

At forty-two, Parth Bhardwaj is an internationally famous author, writing under a pseudonym. Always having steered clear of married women, he has a difficult time keeping away from Anjali, feeling drawn to her from the moment he sets eyes on her.

Just when the two finally realise that they are meant for each other, the unthinkable happens.

Jayant Mathur is found murdered in his bed, making both Parth and Anjali the prime suspects.

Will Anjali ever find happiness in her lonely life?

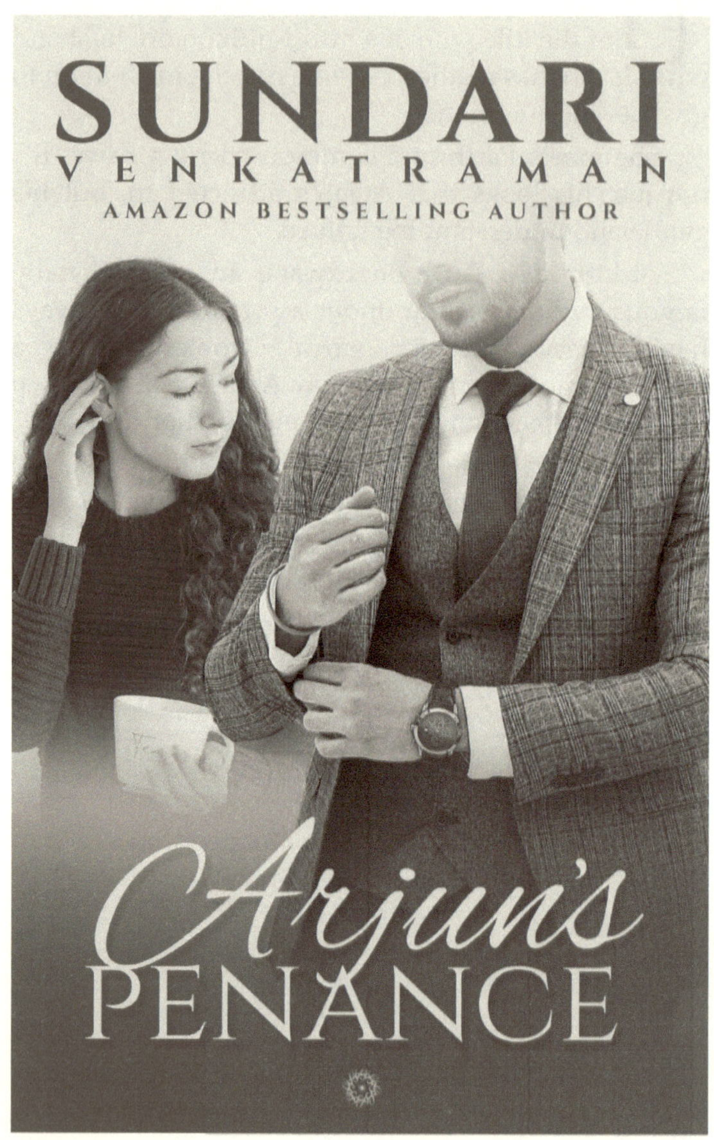

SUNDARI
VENKATRAMAN
AMAZON BESTSELLING AUTHOR
Arjun's
PENANCE

Young Arjun feels betrayed and heartbroken when his girlfriend of two years dies in an accident. In the moment of agony, he does the worst thing possible...

Ten years later, Kiara walks into the office of the Mathur Group of industries, falling for its managing director, Arjun Mathur, who is a ruthless businessman nowadays, and also completely sworn off women.

While the ethical hacker gathers evidence against the ex-finance director of the company who has been swindling money bigtime, she tries to woo the MD into falling in love with her.

Will Kiara be able to persuade Arjun to break his penance?

Connect with Sundari Venkatraman here:

Sundari Venkatraman Books

Sundari Venkatraman Books

https://www.sundarivenkatraman.in

Author Sundari Venkatraman

@sundarivenkat

@sundarivenkatraman

sundarivenkat@gmail.com

www.ingramcontent.com/pod-product-compliance
Lightning Source LLC
Chambersburg PA
CBHW031551150726
47990CB00001B/300